W9-BIW-508

EDITH OLIVIER

was born in the Rectory at Wilton, Wiltshire, in the late 1870s. Her father was Rector there and later Canon of Salisbury. She came from an old Huguenot family which had been living in England for several generations, and was one of a family of ten children. She was educated at home until she won a scholarship to St Hugh's College, Oxford. Her first novel, *The Love Child*, was published in 1927 and there followed four works of fiction: *As Far as Jane's Grandmother's* (1928), *The Triumphant Footman* (1930), *Dwarf's Blood* (1930) and *The Seraphim Room* (1932). Her works of non-fiction were *The Eccentric Life of Alexander Cruden* (1934), *Mary Magdalen* (1934), *Country Moods and Tenses* (1941), *Four Victorian Ladies of Wiltshire* (1945), *Night Thoughts of a Country Lady* (1945), her autobiography, *Without Knowing Mr. Walkley* (1938) and, posthumously published, *Wiltshire* (1951).

Edith Olivier spent her life within twenty miles of her childhood home, and died in her beloved Wilton in 1948.

The Love Child

EDITH OLIVIER

With a New Introduction by
HERMIONE LEE

Published by VIRAGO Limited 1981
Ely House, 37 Dover Street,
London W1X 4HS

First published in Great Britain 1927
by Secker & Warburg Ltd.

Printed in Hong Kong by
Colorcraft Limited

British Library Cataloguing in Publication Data

Olivier, Edith
The love child
(Virago modern classic)
I. Title
823'.9'1F PR6029.L53/

ISBN 0-86068-168-8

Introduction

The Love Child, part fantasy, part social comedy, part psychological study, is an oddity. Its prim, stiff manner, its matter-of-factness, its period quality and its narrow focus are deceptive. The novel's quiet, edgy negotiation between the real and the fictive seems unexpectedly modern; out of the old-fashioned rectitude emerges a disconcerting story of neurotic repression and possessiveness.

The strangeness of *The Love Child* is to some extent explained by the story of Edith Olivier's family life. She was one of the youngest of a clergyman's family of ten children. She grew up in the Rectory at Wilton, and in Salisbury Close. After her father's death she lived with her sister Mildred, and then alone, in the "Daye" (Dairy) House on the Earl of Pembroke's estate at Wilton Park. In the 1890s she went to what was then St Hugh's Hall, Oxford, for four terms on a Bishop Wordsworth Scholarship to read history, but the rest of her life was spent in Wiltshire. She was an officer in the Womens' Land Army in the First War, and three times Mayor of Wilton during the Second War. She had a "circle" – Rex Whistler, who illustrated several of her books, was a close friend, and David Cecil, Siegfried Sassoon, Stephen Tennant, Osbert Sitwell and Brian Howard are among those mentioned fondly in her autobiography. Sydney Olivier, the

Fabian, was her cousin; another cousin, Tom Hunt, was an admiral; one brother became Rural Dean of Chigwell; others went into the army. She wrote five novels, a children's story, a cookery book, an anecdotal autobiography, a couple of lightweight biographies (one a life of Mary Magdalen), a few "pen portraits" – of her sister Mildred, of Victorian "ladies of leisure" – and some books about Wiltshire. She died in 1948 – having refused to reveal her date of birth, which must have occurred in 1879, for *Who's Who*. She looks, in short, like the "typical" late-Victorian country lady and *belle lettriste*, with family and friends in the upper (and predominantly right-wing)echelons of English society.

Nevertheless, there is a not quite usual, even alarming quality to her descriptions of life at Wilton. Canon Dacre Olivier (1881-1919), who was of French Huguenot stock, and whose formidable mother insisted on all three of her sons becoming clergymen, was an austere, autocratic idealist, a man of strong emotions and "military self-control", who organised his parish and his family life along the same rigorous lines. "He expected his sons and daughters to adopt his own peculiar rule of life, and he used no persuasion to dispose them to this. He commanded." He was a fanatical traditionalist with "a great sense of ecclesiastical dignity", who kept up an elaborate style of living in spite of his natural asceticism and the heavy cost of his house and his sons' education at public schools. His daughters were all educated at home, first by their mother ("a wife of the old school" who "had no life outside her husband's"), later by a governess. Their lives were tied to the home ("he would never allow his daughters to be away . . . on any of the great Church festivals"), their conversation was regulated by his standards ("nothing must be spoken of, of which he did not approve"), and he was equally opposed to the idea of their having a career or getting married. It was a highly formalised life. Until they were eighteen, the daughters had to curtsey to their parents on entering the drawing-room. No one went out after dinner, meals and prayers were always at fixed times, and every summer morning the girls arranged the flowers (roses were the Canon's greatest passion) in the Rectory Hall:

> Although he always sat alone in the study, he liked us within call. He hated anyone in the house going out to parties. The comings and goings worried him. He was truly conservative. As the family party had been yesterday, so he wished it to be today, and tomorrow, and so on *ad infinitum*.

The two youngest daughters, Edith and Mildred, led a peculiar secret and intimate existence within, but slightly apart from the family, playing endlessly at the kinds of imaginary games which gave rise to and characterise the relationship of Agatha and Clarissa in *The Love Child*. Mildred, a semi-invalid whose life was even more enclosed than Edith's (she hated train journeys and refused to go to dances) looked after the Canon between the mother's death in 1912 and his in 1919. He was a difficult patient; after his death Mildred herself was "never really well again", and became increasingly dependent on Edith. A friend, Pamela Grey, reminiscing in the sentimental little memorial volume published privately after Mildred's death, remembers that Mildred (like Agatha with Clarissa) "would agonize if this most beloved sister was out even walking down the village street, beyond her sight". About a year and a half after Mildred's death and the compilation of the memorial volume, Edith quite suddenly began *The Love Child*, writing two chapters in one night, at high speed and in an almost trance-like state of mind. Evidently the story of the imaginary child, invented for company by a lonely woman, who can be seen and loved by others, but who must belong wholly to her creator, or she will disappear, arises directly out of the loss of her sister. But Canon Olivier and the Wilton childhood also play their part in the novel.

In her autobiography and her Wiltshire books, Edith Olivier expresses an enthusiasm for her father's system, and for a traditional rural way of life. She is grateful, she says, for having been kept at home.

> The consequence of the various 'inhibitions'. . . which he laid upon our youthful ambitions, has been for me a happy life spent, not upon the stage or in any of the other professions which presented themselves, not as a wife, mother, mother-in-law, and grandmother (the fate of most of my friends) but as a lifelong inhabitant of Wiltshire, which is in my eyes, the most beautiful of the English counties.

She laments the passing of the "regulated existence" of Victorian country families; she contends that the domestic education of women in the nineteenth century made them "more cultured than the women of today"; she has a generalised dislike for the pace of modern (and especially urban) life; and she repeatedly affirms that her father's system "*worked*". "Fashions and opinions may change, the world look this way and that, uncertain whether to believe or how to act, but within those impenetrable walls, life goes on as before."

But those expressions of placid conservativism are not the whole story. There is a curious split in Edith Olivier's work, suggested by the odd title of her autobiography, *Without Knowing Mr Walkley*, which places the emphasis *not* on rural pleasures at the Rectory, but on her thwarted ambition to become an actress (and thereby to know Mr Walkley, the drama critic of *The Times*). And there is a marked ambivalence in the treatment of the disciplinarians who keep appearing in her novels. *As Far as Jane's Grandmother's* (1928), her second novel, is dominated by the autocratic Mrs Basildon, who prevents her orphaned granddaughter Jane from marrying and, eventually, from taking the veil. Jane, compliant, nervous, and full of admiration for "her grandmother's unchanging purpose in life, and her sure achievement", takes to wearing a hair shirt, and after her grandmother's death, finds herself at thirty-five for the first time "expected to make decisions and to give orders". She becomes, like Agatha, increasingly censorious and prudish: it's apparent that she's missed any chance of happiness and is turning into a lesser version of her grandmother.

The Seraphim Room (1932) presents Canon Olivier as the Reverend Mr Chilvester, twice-married, tyrannical father of half-sisters, one a reclusive invalid artist, the other a more frivolous "modern" type. Canon Olivier's fanatical traditionalism is made fun of in Dean Chilvester's refusal to have drains installed in Chilvester House; his strict authority over his daughters is grotesquely caricatured. Here, one of the daughters has fainted at table:

> Mr Chilvester, who had waited a few seconds for a reply to his last remark, looked enquiringly towards his daughter's place, and she was not to be seen. It gave him a shock, for no-one came and went in his presence with such undue precipitancy. It seemed to him incredible that the girl could have rushed from the room without any apology.

Both Mrs Basildon and Dean Chilvester go slightly mad at the end of their lives. Elsewhere, too, Olivier shows an interest in split personalities and in the dangerous effects of extreme repressiveness. She wrote a life of Alexander Cruden, the eighteenth century compiler of the definitive Concordance to the Bible who went mad three times: "He was living in two worlds at once, and living intensely in both". She wrote a most peculiar novel called *Dwarf's Blood* about the hereditary split in a family between normal offspring and dwarves. Her "pen portraits" are concerned with double natures: the Wiltshire lady who "possessed two distinct personalities", the day-time landlady and night-time writer; Annie Moberly, the bishop's daughter and first Principal of St Hugh's, who heard voices and saw visions.

The Love Child doubly enacts the idea of possession which came so directly out of Edith Olivier's relationship with her father and her sister. Agatha is "possessed" by her imaginary child, Clarissa; she also possesses her. Agatha's custody of Clarissa – timorous, over-protective, resistant to change – is an intense version of the family despotism under which Edith grew up. At the same time the splitting in two of Agatha into "mother" and "daughter" (an obvious exercise in wish-fulfilment for the childless Edith Olivier) provides a startling metaphor for a repressed self.

There's little mention of the late Mr Bodenham in *The Love Child*, but from the description of his study ("more or less shut up" since his death, with, for Agatha, an aura of "sacredness") it's evident that the reserved, dull lives of Agatha and her mother have been spent under his shadow. Agatha is indecisive, woolly-minded, "slow to formulate her thoughts"; the only definite interest she has ever had was the imaginary child, quashed by a "caustic" governess and now re-invented as a consolation for her mother's death. What begins as a night-time indulgence (described in apparently ingenuous sexual language: "she found herself looking for-ward to bedtime as if something wonderful was going to happen") becomes part of "real" life when Clarissa begins to be visible, not just to Agatha but to servants and visitors. While Clarissa's appearances are intermittent, they are socially distressing (in rather the way that Miss Arkwright is distrubed by the intrusion of a child familiar in Angus Wilson's story "A Little Companion"): "It was terribly embarrassing not to know whether they saw her as one person or two." But once Clarissa's child-presence is established it becomes a consolation to Miss Bodenham. This part of the novel, describing their games together, is particularly interesting for its presentation of Clarissa as the child that Agatha might have been, were it not for her upbringing. Clarissa is greedy, where Agatha has had to "eradicate" her love of sweet things; she has a taste for bright coloured clothes, whereas Agatha had always dressed like her mother; she rummages through the books which Mr Bodenham had forbidden Agatha to read; she likes animals and other children, who had always made Agatha "feel inferior".

As Clarissa grows up, these antitheses become painful to Agatha. Clarissa wants to learn to drive, to go dancing, to play tennis (though she does none of these social activities conventionally) while Agatha is anxious to protect and prevent her. The opposition is summed up by their different attitudes to game-playing:

> Agatha had enjoyed the acting games, in which she and Clarissa passed practically the whole of their lives, because, through all the stirring adventures that they imagined together, there ran the serene certainty that they were all the while in a world where the events were entirely under control . . . Clarissa, on the other hand, had found in them her nearest point of contact with the real world of adventure.

The "real world of adventure" means falling in love with a man; so the conflict between the safety of fantasy and the dangers of reality turns into a sexual conflict, in which Clarissa is predictably destroyed.

As Agatha tries to fight off Clarissa's lover, she becomes increasingly grotesque and neurotic and is seen through the eyes of Clarissa's "modern" young friends as an insufferably old-fashioned and over-protective figure. Here she prepares for a drive to a picnic:

> Agatha took many rugs, mackintoshes, cushions, furs, and scarves: two camp stools, two white parasols lined with green, as well as a kettle and baskets of food. She prepared for any vagaries of the weather, and she wore goloshes, spectacles of tinted glass, and a large blue veil tied over her head.

This repressed and repressive character is the novel's best feature. Her awkward attempts to bring Clarissa within the pale of law and religion, her horror of motor-cars, her sick headaches, are at once poignant and absurd. The most disconcerting scene in the novel, Clarissa's adoption of a pet monkey, "Poppet", which is like a "diabolical caricature" of the child, brilliantly displays Agatha's inhibitions, while serving as a bizarre parody of the whole plot:

> It was a whirlwind in her sedate house . . . It knew no law and obeyed no authority. Agatha hated its hideous, miserable, grinning human face, which seemed to her to degrade the race of man, dragging it down toward its own apish level.

This is the dark side of Agatha's night-time imaginings. What she has brought into being is not, however, a monstrous dwarf or monkey but a frail, pretty child. Clarissa's romantic quality is, in fact, rather indulged by the novel, and the love affair is soft stuff. It is Canon Olivier, and his stifling of his daughters' lives, who provides the novel's strongest inspiration, and not the delicate Mildred.

Whether Clarissa's name was chosen as a tribute to *Mrs Dalloway* (1925) I don't know; Edith Olivier might well have had in mind the split in that novel between madness and the "social" self. The more obvious influences, here as elsewhere in her work, are Jane Austen (Agatha becomes increasingly like a female version of Mr Woodhouse) and Nathaniel Hawthorne (Clarissa running about the garden in her bright clothes is reminiscent of Pearl in *The Scarlet Letter*). *The Love Child* is, also, very much of its time: fantasy stories like Sylvia Townsend Warner's *Lolly Willowes* (1926) and David Garnett's *Lady into Fox* (1922) were popular. But the search for influences and analogues is not a very useful one. *The Love Child*, though slight, is an extremely unusual novel, not easy to categorise or to forget.

Hermione Lee, University of York 1980

References are made to the following works by Edith Olivier:

Mildred (1926); *The Love Child* (1927, first repr. 1951); *As Far as Jane's Grandmother's* (1928); *Dwarf's Blood* (1931); *The Seraphim Room* (1932); *The Eccentric Life of A. Cruden* (1934); *Mary Magdalen* (1934); *Without Knowing Mr Walkley* (1938); *Country Moods and Tenses* (1941); *Night Thoughts of a Country Landlady* (1943); *Four Victorian ladies of Wiltshire* (1945); *Wiltshire* (1951).

I

Agatha Bodenham had unconsciously moved a pace or two from the others, and she stood, isolated, near the head of her mother's grave while the clergyman finished the service. She was wearing a dress of the shape and the tone of black which her dressmaker thought suitable for mourning orders, and her hat was quite without character. She did not cry, though her veil fluttered a little, as if her breath came uncertainly, and it was wet where a sudden gasp had drawn it into her mouth. Her face was expressionless—with a lack of expression so complete as to suggest more surely than the most speaking countenance an utter and irremediable loneliness—a loneliness that could not be broken, because it meant that she simply hadn't got the power of getting into touch with her fellow-creatures. Perhaps Agatha felt nothing. Certainly she could never tell what she felt, nor ask and receive sympathy.

Cousin Louisa was a kind woman. She watched Agatha standing there, and she felt it was impossible to go back to London that afternoon with the various other distant relatives with whom she had travelled down to attend Mrs. Bodenham's funeral. That forlorn figure appealed to her.

So when they were back at the house, she came to Agatha and said:

"I want you to let me stay with you for a night or two, dear. We can't leave you quite alone."

Agatha was faintly surprised, and mostly because Cousin Louisa called her "dear." She had only seen her once before, and that was a long time ago.

But her face, which had expressed no grief,

now expressed neither surprise, pleasure, nor annoyance. She concluded that this was what happened at funerals, and she ordered a bedroom to be prepared.

Cousin Louisa stayed two days—two strange, unnatural, gloomy days, and she felt it was no use staying longer.

She knew there was much to be done: Mrs. Bodenham's clothes and personal belongings to be sorted and disposed of; business papers to be dealt with; letters to be answered. But Agatha began none of these things. It seemed to be unfitting to do any of them in the presence of a stranger, and she refused all of her cousin's offers of help.

Cousin Louisa's presence did not make her less desolate: it merely added to her desolation a sense of discomfort. She was not used to having guests, and she did not know how to cope with them; nor did she know whether the servants were annoyed at her having one in the house. The two women sat awkwardly together, searching for things to say; they took short walks together—objectless walks on roads leading nowhere in particular: they parted at night with relief, after sitting face to face for an hour after dinner, furtively watching the hands of the clock moving minute by minute towards the bedtime hour of ten; and when they finally parted for good, each breathed more freely.

Yet as Agatha sat in the drawing-room that evening after dinner, she realized that though she was glad to be without Cousin Louisa, she did feel terribly lonely. It was her first night alone.

Strange that she should feel it so, for she had always been solitary—a solitary child, a solitary girl, and now, at thirty-two, a still more solitary woman.

She and her mother were women of peculiarly reserved natures, finding it hard to make friends, and holding their country neighbours at a distance. So reserved, too, that they had been barely intimate with each other, living through their days side by side without real mingling of experiences or sharing of confidences. Indeed, they had neither experiences nor confidences to share.

The truth was that the Bodenhams were dull. The neighbours found them so, and by degrees people had come less and less to the house; and they found each other so, although perhaps unconsciously. Yet even a dull woman can be lonely, and this was what Agatha felt as she sat by the fire that night.

Now that Cousin Louisa had gone, the house seemed very empty. She missed the sound of Mrs. Bodenham's footsteps, the clatter of her knife and fork at dinner, and the click of her knitting needles in the evening.

She was always slow to formulate her thoughts, which generally slid shapelessly about in the background of her mind, never expecting to find themselves clothed in words. Now, sitting among the half-tones of her musings, Agatha slowly became aware that once before she had felt this same sense of loneliness. Her life, which seemed never to have had anything in it, had yet already, at some time or another, been emptied as it was to-day, and emptied of companionship. She dumbly searched the past.

A name shot across her consciousness, like something suddenly alive—

Clarissa!

Yes: it was Clarissa—forgotten for many years, and now coming back to mind as a memory, not of a possession, but of a loss.

It was so very long ago, and had been nothing but a childish fancy.

Like many other only children, when Agatha was a little girl she had created for herself an imaginary companion, who shared everything with her. Clarissa had been as real as a brother or sister of flesh and blood—and far more amenable—and because of her Agatha had never felt her childhood to be a lonely one. But when she was fourteen years old, her governess had found out about Clarissa, and the caustic drops of Miss Marks' common sense fell like a weed killer upon the one blossom of Agatha's imagination. Clarissa wilted—perished: or rather she was put away out of sight, like other outgrown toys, on the top shelf of the nursery cupboard, "too good" to be given away to the children of the poor.

And now, after eighteen years, Agatha felt once more the same desolation. She felt more moved than she had been at her mother's funeral. There arose in her a spirit of rebellion, a sense of injustice. How dared Miss Marks play the part of a Moloch, and demand from her the sacrifice of her own child? For Clarissa had been alive—more alive to Agatha than any of the real people who had moved about, around her. The creation of Clarissa was the fruit of the one active movement of Agatha's mind. Clarissa had taken shape. She had possessed not only a name, but a personality of her own. She had responded to Agatha's cry for companionship with what had seemed to be a real living voice, and when she had been shamefacedly huddled away, to escape from the satire of Miss Marks, Agatha's mind had become misty and vague, and had grown more so year by year. And as the old memory came back, it seemed to Agatha that in losing Clarissa, she had not only lost a real playmate, but she had also lost the only being who had ever awoken her own personality, and made it responsive—she had lost something without which she had grown as futile as a racket idly striking the air, against no ball.

"I talked to Clarissa," she said to herself, "and I have never really talked to anyone else. She made me think of things to say, and know how to say them. She woke me up; and Miss

Marks stopped all that when she wouldn't allow me to "talk to myself" as she called it. But I really did say things to Clarissa—things that I wanted to say. I knew she understood."

Agatha sat forward in her chair. There was colour in her cheeks. She almost looked animated, amused. Why should she not play with Clarissa again? There was no one now to forbid her talking to herself.

She tried to recapture the old trick. It eluded her. She had lost it. She couldn't the least remember how it was done; and yet it was there, on the threshold of her mind, on the doorstep, so real, and yet just out of reach. She tried to speak to Clarissa, but she couldn't think what to say, or how to say it. No words would come—only the name Clarissa—a little thin streak of moving light that trembled in her dumb darkness. And when she said even the one word "Clarissa" aloud, the sound of her own voice broke the spell woven by her silent thoughts, and shattered the image she was catching at.

Yet she knew that Clarissa could only live—had only lived—in her own power of talking with her.

She got up and walked about, saying the name over and over again, first of all in a whisper, then a little louder, and then louder again. She tried to remind herself of the games she had played with Clarissa. . . . "Do you remember this? . . . Have you forgotten that? . . . What fun we had in the garden on my birthday! . . . And O, Clarissa, how naughty you were when you wouldn't go to church on Easter Sunday!"

Muttering, she began to feel as if it were beginning to come back. She remembered little turns in the game, little secrets she had shared with Clarissa. She heard herself laugh—naturally, clearly, almost loudly.

"Clarissa!" she said again.

The door opened. Helen, the parlour-maid,

came into the room carrying the bedroom candlestick—one solitary candlestick now. The sight of it ought to have brought home to Agatha the fact of her own loneliness; it would have done so an hour ago. But now, instead, she only realized that Helen must have heard her talking to herself.

She walked to the window, drew back the curtain, and stared out into the night. She could see nothing at all, but she didn't want to see anything.

Helen looked at her back with respectful sympathy. Miss Bodenham was acting just as she should. She had been interrupted in a paroxysm of sorrow, which she was trying to conceal by averting her face.

"Try and go on to bed, Miss," she said. "I know what you must be feeling, but you mustn't give way. Time will cure. Shall I make you a nice cup of tea?"

"Thank you, Helen," Agatha answered in

a dull, empty voice, and without turning round. "Yes, I will go upstairs, and it would be nice to have a cup of tea in bed. Very kind of you."

Tears were in her eyes, and her voice broke in its deadness. Helen had spoilt everything. Clarissa had been coming back to life, and so had she herself; but now a door had shut heavily, and she was back again in the half life she had lived for so long, where all voices were muffled, and where no one ever got through to another.

She went upstairs to bed, feeling as if she had caught at a dancing flame, only to find that it had no substance, but had left a burn behind.

II

Clarissa came back in the night.

She moved through Agatha's dreams with all her old individuality, and Agatha dreamt that she was playing with her just as she had done when she was ten years old. But in the morning the mood had passed, and she didn't even want to recall it. Clarissa had the absurdity which often belongs to the remembered dreams that have seemed the most natural when one was asleep. And she would not admit to herself that she had begun trying to play with Clarissa before she even went to bed at all: that memory made her think she must have been a little mad.

She was busy. Now that Cousin Louisa had left her, she set to work on the business which had been awaiting her: she wrote to her lawyer about Probate; she answered letters of condolence; she sorted bundles of Mrs. Bodenham's papers.

Agatha did all this with a kind of second-rate efficiency, uninspired. She seemed to be living in a world of shadows from which had vanished the figures which had thrown those blurred but still moving reflections: in a world of echoes, too faint and remote to convey any of the meaning once expressed by the voices which had called them out of silence, in a world of dying scents, dimly suggesting some memory of a past once alive. But when she tried to connect the vanished presence, the silenced voice, the dying memory, with the figure of her mother, as she thought she ought to do, it seemed to her that Mrs. Bodenham had always been as far away as she was to-day. Hers was not the living personality she missed.

It was last night. It was Clarissa.

She felt guilty and ashamed, and she buried

herself among dusty papers. Clarissa receded, and Agatha felt herself again becoming the Miss Bodenham her maids expected her to be.

She worked steadily for several hours. She ate her meals when they came. She walked in the garden to benefit her digestion.

Her life seemed coated with dust like the papers she handled—the dust of years. It had lain there always, certainly ever since the days of Miss Marks; but now she saw it suddenly, for the first time, lying there thick and grey, giving a dreary sameness to all that it lay upon. It was as if a shaft of light had shot into a darkened room, revealing a cloud of motes, and she knew that Clarissa's name was the ray which had struck across her dusty life.

But Agatha did not again yield to the temptation of talking aloud to Clarissa, indeed, she did not feel it all that day. Life among dusty papers was far more normal.

Nevertheless, she found herself looking forward to bedtime as if something wonderful was going to happen, something which she did not even try to define to herself, for her mind was back in its usual condition, vague and confused. Yet behind all her occupations, her walk and her dinner, a little glow-worm glimmered on her horizon: she did not think about it, but she knew it was there.

And then in the night, as she lay in that half-sleeping state when the spirit wakes because the mind is weary, when impossibilities seem possible, and when dreams come true—then, all of a sudden, she found that she was playing with Clarissa, quite simply and naturally. She had forgotten what fun it was till she did it again, and did it quite easily too, without any of that painful searching and groping about which had teased and distressed her the evening before.

Clarissa hadn't grown a day older, and Agatha found that she could play with her with all the zest and spirit of her own childhood, and yet there was something added. Between her and Clarissa there stood the memory of eighteen middle-aged years, for she knew she had never been young since she lost Clarissa. She felt as if she was playing with a baby, and she knew that the baby was her own.

But in the morning it had all gone, and again she thought it absurd, or she told herself that she thought so. Really she knew that she was only seeking for some way of satisfying herself that it was not absurd at all, but was only natural and normal that now she was alone she should go back in memory to the days of her childhood.

So the next week or two passed. Agatha worked steadily all day, and all night she played with Clarissa. She ceased, in her own mind, to be ashamed of it. She justified it to her common sense by considering that, as other women found their recreation in Society, or in novel reading, or in gossip, so she, who had never been amused by these things, found hers in this creation of her own imagination. But Agatha was glad she was alone in the house: she knew that her explanation would not have satisfied Miss Marks, or Mrs. Bodenham, or even Cousin Louisa.

For by degrees Clarissa became a part of the day, too. Agatha had got completely back into the trick, and just as in the old days, it was again the natural thing to accompany all her doings by an undercurrent of talk with Clarissa. They shared everything together.

Walking in the garden one day, picking a flower now and then and carrying on an intermittent conversation with Clarissa, who insisted on running on to the flower beds and dirtying her red shoes, Agatha was suddenly startled by hearing a little footstep quite close behind her, literally on her heels. She turned round quickly. No one was there. She realized that she had so vividly imagined the little figure leaping around her, that her ear had taken part in the play. And then the garden, all at once, seemed full of little footsteps, and Agatha could hardly believe that it was mere fancy which discovered the print of a tiny foot here and there among the loose soil. But that, of course, was the kind of thing which anyone might imagine anywhere. Still, Agatha again had a frightened suspicion that she was going mad. She pushed the thought away, assuring herself that she was well and sanely aware that Clarissa was only a game: she was in no way an obsession.

Those walks in the garden were the times when Clarissa was most real. Little movements which might have been the scuffling of a squirrel in the branches overhead, or the pit-pat of a bird's hopping feet, or even the stir of a worm in the earth—all these became sound which might well be Clarissa. She ran lightly about the garden; her starched summer dress crackled; she rustled through the bushes; she broke off twigs from the shrubs. Agatha found herself constantly looking sharply round, thinking there was someone behind her.

Then one day, when Agatha was quietly sitting on the white seat at the end of the green walk, darning a black woollen stocking to wear in church the next day, and for once more absorbed in darning than in dreaming—then, all of a sudden, Clarissa came and sat on the seat beside her. She was smaller even than Agatha had imagined her, and she looked young for her age, which must have been ten or eleven. Her hair was brushed off her face and tied back with a brown ribbon, a little darker than the hair, which was dappled, like the skin of a fawn. Her face was tiny, very pale, and her eyes were dappled brown, like her hair. She wore a short white dress of embroidered cambric, and on her feet were the little red shoes which Agatha knew she had always worn. Physically, she looked shadowy and pathetic, but a spirit peeped out of her eyes, with something of roguishness in it. Chastened, subdued roguishness, perhaps, but yet it was unmistakably there.

"I have been with the Bunyans," said Clarissa, "and now Mrs. Bunyan has gone to fetch the milk, so I came here."

The Bunyans were the family of an imaginary gamekeeper, who had always been a part of the Clarissa Game.

Agatha felt as she used to do as a little child, when she was allowed to look at the inside of her father's watch, and was told not to breathe in case she should stop the works.

"I wish you wouldn't be so much with the Bunyans," she answered. "Now you are such a big girl, you ought to be more with me. The Bunyans are not suitable companions."

Clarissa shifted her seat to the arm of the bench.

"Don't scold me," she said, "or I shall go away."

Agatha's heart beat. She was agonized. But an instinct told her that she must not appear too concerned. Fervour would frighten Clarissa.

So she laughed with a duplicity at which she was both surprised and proud.

"You can't really get away from me," she said. "I've got you on a string."

"Try!" said Clarissa. "Catch me if you can."

It was a game after her own heart. She had always loved Touchwood, Tom Tiddler's Ground, and Hide and Seek, and now she jumped off the seat, and stood for a moment just out of reach.

Agatha grabbed at her.

She danced off—only a yard or two, and stood, poised.

Throwing down the woollen stocking,

Agatha was wholeheartedly in the game. She sprang at Clarissa—missed her—and then they ran, one behind the other, laughing, down the path towards the house. Clarissa was fleet of foot, but Agatha's legs were the longer. She gained on her quarry and grabbed at the flying sash . . . she caught it . . . but . . . she could not hold it. It went through her fingers—vanished, and Agatha had, in reaching at it, taken her eyes for just that one second off the little girl herself.

Clarissa disappeared in that second.

She was gone.

Baffled and breathless, Agatha looked about from side to side. There was no one to be seen. The garden lay perfectly quiet around her. She was alone. Then she looked back at the stocking which she had left on the seat. She felt very foolish, and too much ashamed of herself to walk back the length of the path and take up her darning again.

She went into the house, hoping that neither of the servants had seen her racing madly about the garden, pursuing someone whom she realized had not been there at all. They would have thought her mad. And would they be right or wrong?

As usual Agatha did not follow up the train of thought. She was not in the habit of thinking things out.

But after this she often saw Clarissa in the garden. At first she came and went, very suddenly and fleetingly. She jumped in and out of the shrubs and flowers, in one moment beside Agatha, and in the next leaving only the swing of a great peony blossom to show where she had slipped into the herbaceous border. As the days went by, however, she became less shy, and was nearly always there, so that the sight of her was a daily part of the Clarissa Game.

And all the time she was seen by Agatha

alone. To the rest of the world she was entirely invisible.

At first it was difficult to believe this; the appearance was so real. But Agatha discovered it one day when she suddenly saw the gardener watching her playing Touchwood with Clarissa, who was springing about from tree to tree, a most conspicuous figure in the white dress.

For a moment Agatha was aghast, feeling that both the play and the playmate were equally impossible to explain.

"Is it the kitten you be after, Miss?" Hunt asked, as she paused in her pursuit. "Here she be, just skipped up the apple tree right over them rhubarb pots."

So he had not seen Clarissa, and Agatha knew that the little girl could be seen by her eyes alone.

By degrees Clarissa grew less elusive. It was not only in the garden that she appeared; she came into the house. She sat opposite to Agatha at the dining-room table, on the chair vacated by Mrs. Bodenham, looking ridiculously small and incongruous between its wide arms of dark green leather. She played with the contents of Agatha's extremely tidy workbasket on the what-not in the drawing-room, and made a terrible mess of the carefully arranged cottons and silks. And up in the bedroom she took from the hair tidy the "combings" which were accumulating to make a "switch" to be added to Agatha's thinning locks, and threw them out of the window, when they drifted about the garden, and were collected by the birds as linings for nests.

And the servants never saw Clarissa. She fearlessly ran in and out of the garden door, under the very nose of Sarah, the austere and elderly housemaid, who was dusting the hall table. She sat with Agatha behind the tea-tray while Helen carried in the kettle and set it on the stand. When Agatha was being given the cup of warm gruel which she always drank after she got into bed, Clarissa played with the trinkets on the dressing-table and made such a noise among the rings, that Helen looked sharply round to see what was happening and then walked gravely across the room, and closed the window to keep out the draught.

III

Clarissa was very fond of raspberries. Agatha was picking for jam, and Clarissa, by way of helping her, hovered around, eating all the biggest fruit in the basket, and she picked a great many for herself and ate them before they ever reached thc basket at all.

She was certainly greedy.

Agatha wondered why. She remembered with some embarrassment that food had once been her own secret delight; that cakes and puddings had been the great events of her days, until this degraded taste was slowly eradicated by years of good manners and bad cooking.

But in any case she could not be severe with Clarissa, not even when she crushed a big raspberry on to the front of her one white dress, and made an ugly stain right down it.

She looked less fragile and shadowy too when her face and hands were stained with crimson juice—in fact she was a real little ragamuffin that morning.

So normal had her presence become, that Agatha for some moments was vaguely listening to her chattering away with Reggie the garden boy before it dawned upon her what was happening.

Clarissa was becoming visible to other people. Agatha was shaken.

She heard Reggie pointing out a very large and ripe raspberry to Clarissa, and then she heard him quickly add:

"Here's Miss Bodenham, I must hop it."

Agatha looked stately. She could do this with a garden boy.

"Who are you speaking to?" she asked.

Reggie looked about him, completely puzzled.

"The young lady was here just now," he said, "but she's gone again."

As a matter of fact, Clarissa was standing quite conspicuously only a yard or two away from him, in the very act of putting into her mouth the very large raspberry he had pointed out. She looked triumphant and mischievous.

Agatha told Reggie to go and help the gardener mow the lawn. She was terribly agitated. The situation was growing beyond her control. If Clarissa appeared to the outer world she would have to be explained. This in itself was difficult enough; but if her appearances were to become disappearances while they were in the very process of being explained, the situation was more than difficult, it was impossible.

Old Hunt saw her the next day. He asked Agatha to tell the young lady not to run about over the radish bed, where he had just put in the seed.

Agatha answered him faintly. Panic slowly

mounted within her. She was almost beside herself. Clarissa was growing unmanageable. What was to be said to Helen or Sarah if the child were seen in the house, and she certainly would be, sooner or later. For she was here, there, and . . . nowhere, and there seemed to be no possible way of telling whether she was visible or not. Agatha felt she dared not appear before her own servants, not knowing whether to their eyes she would be alone or accompanied by a strange child.

She hurried away when she heard anyone coming. She walked in the shrubbery, out of sight of the house. She hid in a corner till she heard Helen shut the kitchen door after bringing the tea into the drawing-room, and then she went in, and hastily ate a furtive meal, with Clarissa curled up on the sofa beside her. After tea she hurried back to the shrubbery and wandered among the bushes. Frantic plans were forming in her mind. She knew that she must come to grips with the situation and immediately. With every hour that passed she realized that her odd behaviour was more and more likely to excite question. She could not spend the rest of her life hiding among the laurels in the garden.

She went to bed before dinner.

Firmly taking Clarissa by the scruff of the neck, she forced her into her own bed, pushed her under the sheets, and held her there while she rang the bell and parleyed with Helen, telling her that she did not feel well, and would dine in bed. And then she added:

"I think I want a change. I shall go to Brighton to-morrow."

Agatha had never before in all her life made a sudden decision. She never left home. She knew that this move on her part would astonish the household, filling the kitchen with voluble surmise. This idea was distasteful, more than distasteful, it was alarming. But the possible discovery of Clarissa was still more alarming—the discovery of a Clarissa who could not be relied on from one moment to another, and of whom, more literally than of Shakespeare, it might be said:

"Others abide our question. Thou art free."

Clarissa certainly could not be counted on to "abide"—either question or answer. She came and went, free as air.

Agatha left by the early train next day. The morning was a short one, but it held an eternity of torture.

The servants were in and out of her room every minute, helping to pack, asking for instructions on this detail and on that, arranging, disarranging, asking for money, for her address in Brighton (which she didn't know), for the possible length of her stay (which she knew still less). And all the time Clarissa was in and out too, sending Agatha into a fever. Every now and then, she was sure that she caught the damp green eye of Sarah fixed on the child; and a minute or two later Helen's alert ear appeared to hear the sound of her movements in the room. But no questions were asked, and there was no doubt that the sudden apparition of an unaccountable child in the room would not have passed without comment.

Another cause of anxiety was Clarissa's white cambric dress. It was not suitable for a train journey, and if she became visible in the railway carriage the other passengers would certainly wonder at her being so unsuitably dressed. So Agatha decided to carry with her a plaid shawl which had belonged to Mrs. Bodenham, and this could be wrapped round Clarissa to cover her thin dress in the train.

The cab came at ten. The servants clustered round, with bags, hold-alls, parcels, and sandwiches. Agatha stepped in and sat down, with Clarissa beside her, demure and quiet for once.

Agatha could hardly believe that no one could see the little girl, but she was undoubtedly invisible, for Helen brought out the dressing-case at the last moment, and placed it on the seat beside Agatha, exactly on to Clarissa's lap. Agatha sprang forward instinctively, putting out her hand to save the child. Her alarm was quite unnecessary, for the dressing-case fell solidly through Clarissa on to the seat beneath her, and she was obviously none the worse.

But Agatha had come to the end of her nerves, and this last episode was too much for her. She burst into hysterical laughter.

Helen, Sarah, and the Cook were already very anxious over the sudden and unprecedented journey which their mistress was taking alone; and now this unexpected fit of laughter, so unlike her, and so uncalled for, showed that she must indeed be in a very unnatural state.

"Are you sure that you are up to the journey, Miss?" Helen asked, pausing before she got out of the cab, and laying an affectionate hand on Agatha's gloved one. "We don't like you going away by yourself like this. It doesn't seem right. Won't you wait till the next train, and let me get ready and come with you? I know you would find me useful, all by yourself in one of them great hotels."

Agatha was touched. She disliked the thought of appearing unappreciative of the affection for herself which she felt existed in all her servants, but to take either of them with her was, of course, an impossibility. It was to escape them that she was going away.

"Thank you, Helen," she said kindly. "It is very good of you to think of it, but I want you all to have a rest and a quiet time for a while. I shall perhaps send for you later on, but not yet."

And she ordered the cabman to drive on.

Agatha travelled first class, and alone with Clarissa, who shivered and felt cold. She was ill at ease on the journey, as Agatha was herself. She was glad she had thought of bringing the plaid, and she pinned it rather awkwardly round Clarissa, who seemed grateful for it, and nestled into the corner of the carriage, holding it up to her chin. She looked a very funny little thing, and not a bit like herself, as she stepped wearily out of the train when at last they got to Brighton. The voluminous folds of the shawl were dragging all round her in the dust of the platform, and she almost looked a dull and dirty child.

But no sooner was she out of the carriage than she became herself again. She frisked away from Agatha, absolutely refusing to take her hand, gave a little kick, which released her from the plaid and its safety pins, and skipped off in her white dress to watch the luggage being taken out of the van.

Agatha picked up the shawl and followed, but she could not persuade Clarissa to let her pin it round her again. She said she was quite warm and didn't want it.

They drove to a hotel, the name of which Agatha had remembered because she had once heard of somebody who had stayed there.

It looked very large and modern, and Agatha was rather overwhelmed by the reception given her by the *maître d'hôtel*, manageress, page boys, and boots, who all seemed to be helping her out of the cab and into the hall.

She led Clarissa by the hand, trying to keep her own hand in a position which would look natural, whether a small girl were attached to it or not.

She watched the eyes of the hotel people. It was terribly embarrassing not to know whether they saw her as one person or as two.

Agatha engaged a bedroom and a private sitting-room, asking for a room with two beds, "As my little niece—will stay with me for part of my visit."

It was with an almost piteous appeal in her eyes that, as she spoke, she watched the face of the most agreeable and courteous manageress, trying to judge from her expression whether the little niece was seen to be beside her or not.

She thought not, for though the woman looked as though she liked children, a kind motherly face, she never gave a glance in the direction of Clarissa, but led Agatha upstairs, and showed her into a most comfortable little suite on the first floor. Clarissa ran about the room, looking at everything, and was delighted when she found that the window opened on to a balcony, and looked out upon the sea.

Agatha cut short the conversation of the manageress, and rather hurried her out of the room. It was evident that Clarissa was as yet invisible, but she dreaded every moment that the child might suddenly be seen by the woman, without any possibility of her entrance upon the scene being naturally explained.

When they were alone, she took Clarissa on to her knee, and together they looked out of the window.

It was a wonderful moment. Agatha had never felt so free in all her life. She and Clarissa were alone together at the seaside. Nobody knew them. No one would question them. In the crowded hotel, Clarissa could come and go as she pleased, and Agatha need explain nothing. She could live in each moment as it came.

She held Clarissa's hand and rubbed it gently.

"I wish I could make your little hand feel warm," she said. "It is always cold."

"It will soon be warm here," said Clarissa, and she held it out towards the sun.

It was very transparent.

IV

Agatha marvelled at herself during those first weeks at Brighton. She was a completely new creature. It seemed to her that until now she had lived entirely without volition, everything which she did each day being the inevitable consequence of an exactly similar thing which she had done the day before. Such little stupid things, too. And yet she had thought that they must always be done; or rather, she hadn't thought about them at all, but had submitted to them as they came up for doing as if they were the living agents and she merely their passive tool.

Now she came and went just as her fancy took her. Not that Agatha's fancy was likely to take her very far, but the mere fact that she and Clarissa could walk in and out of the hotel unquestioned gave her an unwonted sense of independence. She took care not to talk to Clarissa in the hall or public sitting-rooms, in case at the moment the child happened to be invisible except to her own eyes, as she did not wish to run the risk of getting the character of talking to herself; but except for that precaution she found that it didn't matter a bit whether Clarissa could be seen or not. She could appear and disappear as abruptly as she liked. Nobody noticed. And in their own sitting-room alone, or on the crowded beach, Agatha and Clarissa grew every day more delightfully intimate.

One of the first things they did was to buy new clothes for the little girl. Agatha went to several different shops and ordered boxes of dresses and hats to be sent to the hotel for Clarissa to try on. She dared not risk doing this in a shop, for fear the child should vanish suddenly, either leaving an empty dress suspended in mid air with nobody inside it, or else possibly carrying off with her some garment which was in process of being put on.

Agatha had at first been afraid that Clarissa might refuse to wear anything except the white cambric dress in which she had at first appeared. But no. She was enchanted at the sight of her new clothes, and she loved trying on one thing after another. Agatha bought a great deal. Clothes for herself had always bored her. Everything she had ever worn had been made by the dressmaker who had dressed her mother before her, and the woman's taste had seemed to Agatha as inevitable as a wet day. It was amazing to find herself freely choosing and buying things out of boxes.

And Clarissa had distinct and very decided tastes of her own. This was a comfort to Agatha, who was inclined to turn the things over and over again, quite unable to make up her mind as to which she liked best, or whether she really liked any of them at all. Clarissa knew in a moment. She liked colours, though not very bright ones—green, and a rather deep yellow, and brown. She would have absolutely nothing to say to the white dresses which Agatha vaguely felt were perhaps the best taste for a child of her age. But when she put on the little coloured tunics and straight short dresses there was no doubt that they suited to perfection her very tiny figure and little pointed face. Agatha was reminded of some pictures of elves and fairies which she had loved as a child in a book of fairy stories given to her by her father, and still her most distinct memory of him.

After that, Clarissa would never again put on her old clothes. And from the day that she began to wear the new ones she lost her trick of disappearing. There was never again any question as to whether she was visible or not: she was there beside Agatha for all the world to see, and she was as real to the rest of the world as she was to Agatha herself.

The hotel servants all made friends with her, calling her "an old-fashioned little thing," and so indeed she was. The toys of ordinary children did not amuse her at all: she could not play with them, and she wanted nothing but to be with Agatha and to play at acting games with her. They played at being all sorts of people, but most of all they played at being themselves. They liked this best. Agatha found herself pretending with Clarissa that they two were doing most unexpected things, and finding themselves in situations which would have been very unpleasant in real life, but which were extremely amusing as games. They were suddenly without any money at all, and obliged to sing in the streets, and to sell primroses for a living: or they were on a desert island, eating quantities of the most delicious fruits, which they found growing there: or they had made friends with some of the other people in the hotel (a thing which was really quite impossible for either of them), and they were entertaining a party of these people in Agatha's sitting-room.

Every morning they sat on the beach, and as Agatha watched Clarissa, she saw her becoming daily less frail and shadowy in appearance. There was more colour in her skin: there was a touch of brown in it, and sometimes even of pink, when the sun shone and the wind blew in off the sea. Agatha herself glowed with reflected sunshine at the sight.

All the other children on the beach were busy with spades and buckets, so Agatha bought some, but Clarissa didn't at all know how to play with them, nor had Agatha the least idea how to teach her. They took the spades and buckets conscientiously down to the shore where they dug formally and awkwardly, side by side, each for the sake of the other, and both very bored and unnatural. Agatha was almost in tears, feeling that it must be her fault, and that if she knew more about children she would be able to inspire Clarissa to make sand-castles in the same absorbed way that the other children did. She became exasperated with the spade and bucket for failing to create their own mood and atmosphere, but she was afraid to show exasperation. This was partly because she was not in the habit of expressing her emotions, but it was still more because of the fear, which was always with her, that any sudden movement from her might frighten Clarissa away. She still felt as if she were making friends with a very shy little wild bird, who must not on any account be startled. So she jumped with a pang of shocked delight when Clarissa herself one day suddenly stamped her feet, seized the spade and bucket, and hurled them violently into the sea, as far as her small strength would send them. The next wave tossed them back at her feet. Clarissa picked them up, and once again she flung them into the water; then, without waiting for a moment, she turned and fled. Agatha raced after her, horrified, enchanted, and so absorbed in the pursuit that she was quite unaware of the impression she made upon the people sitting on the beach, as she skipped over sand-castles and dived among deck-chairs in her pursuit of the elfin, impish little girl in her short dress of dark green linen.

When she caught Clarissa, they sat on a breakwater and played at being Punch and Judy. Agatha never tried a spade and bucket again, nor did she buy dolls or any other toys for the little girl. They bored her. Agatha was Clarissa's only toy, and she was Agatha's.

V

Miss Bodenham gave much thought and care to the letter which she wrote to Helen announcing her intention of returning home. She had been nearly three months at Brighton, free and unquestioned, and she had grown so used to having Clarissa with her that she had almost forgotten that the child had not yet been introduced to the servants. But Agatha was beginning to feel homesick. Hotel life was really very uncongenial to her. Its noise and movement wearied her, and she longed to be with Clarissa in her own home, and in the garden where her eyes had first rested on that beloved little form.

But before she reached this haven she had got to account for Clarissa. Agatha was a reserved woman, and she had an innate dislike of the unusual. It was quite impossible for her to tell anyone that Clarissa was nothing but a toy child of her own making. Moreover, her own common sense told her that no person with equal common sense would for a moment believe such a story. She hardly believed it herself when she thought about it. She just didn't think about it at all—she lived, and for the first time in her life. After all, who can explain his own presence on this earth? So why expect anyone to be able to explain the presence of another.

Still, Clarissa's arrival must be prepared for. Agatha did the obvious thing: she always did.

"I intend to return next Saturday," she wrote, "and I shall be very glad to be at home once more. I am bringing a little girl with me, a distant connection of the family, whom I mean to adopt. I know that you will all be glad that I should have this little companion as an interest in my life, and shall not be lonely any more, so that I rely on you to welcome this little orphan and help me to make her happy. Her name is Miss Clarissa Bodenham, and she is eleven years old. I have ordered a small bedstead for her, and this will arrive by goods train before the end of the week. I should like it to be erected in the corner of my own room before we arrive. Miss Clarissa has shared my room here, and I wish this to continue."

It seemed a most ordinary and natural announcement to make, so Agatha thought as she read the letter over, but the word "orphan" made her pause. She was a truthful woman.

Clarissa enjoyed everything, and she was delighted to hear that they were going home. But she hated being kissed by the manageress and the chamber-maid when they said good-bye, and she ducked her head and turned away her face with unconcealed distaste, holding on to Agatha's hand with a return of her old shyness. Agatha was sorry that these kind women should be snubbed in this way, and their affection for Clarissa gratified her, but, nevertheless, she was inwardly delighted by the child's fastidiousness. Clarissa was her own. Hers only.

Miss Bodenham's servants thought that she had certainly done the right thing in adopting a child. They had been thoroughly frightened by that hysterical outburst of hers as she was starting for Brighton, and had feared that she might be becoming "queer." The presence of a child in the house was just what was wanted. So both Agatha and Clarissa received a most cordial welcome when they reached home. Helen and Sarah declared that they could see the likeness to Miss Bodenham when she was a little girl, and they said that anyone could tell that Miss Clarissa was one of the family. This was a subject which Agatha did not pursue, and she quickly changed the conversation by asking whether the bedstead had arrived and what blankets had been put on to it. Everything was ready: Clarissa's bed and her niche in the house were waiting for her as if she had always lived there.

Agatha was amazed to find how easy it was to do an unprecedented thing. Inwardly, she was proud of the way in which she had handled what really was the only event which had happened in her life: and, as she thought to herself, it was an event which would have put the most experienced person into something of a quandary—quite out of the ordinary. Yet here was she, Agatha Bodenham, producing an entirely unexplainable child of eleven years old, and producing her with such an air that no one even thought that an explanation was needed.

She never left Clarissa alone. The child seemed in every way perfectly normal, and Agatha herself often forgot that she wasn't, and yet she could not altogether banish from her mind the uneasy feeling that Clarissa's existence depended on her own immediate presence—that if you happened to find the child alone, you just wouldn't find her at all. It sounded like a paradox, but Agatha could not express it in any other way. Sometimes she thought she would carry out a test, and send Clarissa upstairs on a message, then casually ask Helen to run up and see if Miss Clarissa was in her bedroom or not. But she was afraid. Such a trick seemed disloyal, and it might drive Clarissa away as magically as she had come.

Every morning they did lessons together. Clarissa learnt to read far more quickly than Agatha herself had done. It seemed to come by instinct, and once having learnt, she delighted in books, rummaging about the book-cases, and finding all sorts of attractive old volumes which had belonged to Mr. Bodenham, and which had never been disturbed since his death. Agatha had longed to take them out of the shelves when she was a little girl, but they had been forbidden, and by the time she was old enough to read what she liked the taste had gone.

So when Clarissa found her way into the study, Agatha remembered her own frustrated longings, and hadn't got the heart to say the books were unsuitable. Besides, as she reminded herself, never having opened them, she could not honestly say whether they were suitable or not.

Clarissa therefore read what she liked, and she told Agatha the stories she read—Fielding, Richardson, Scott, Dickens, and Thackeray. She read much poetry aloud—Crabbe, Byron, Southey, Wordsworth, and Tennyson. Mr. Bodenham's library was a conventional one. It contained only standard works, and no addition had been made to it since his death.

One day Clarissa found on an upper shelf the two small leather-bound volumes of a book called *Sturm's Reflections*. They were filled with somewhat didactic religious meditations, arranged in a series of readings for every day in the year, and dealing with such subjects as the Wonders of Nature, the Discoveries of Science, and the History and Characteristics of the Peoples of the Globe. The book was completely abreast of the scientific thought of 1817, the year in which it was published, and its tone was religiously and sanely orthodox. Oddly enough, both Agatha and Clarissa were entranced with it. Agatha was at rest among its platitudes, while its scientific tone made her feel in touch with the spirit of the age: and Clarissa delighted in the author's erratic way of leaping about from Laplanders to comets, and from earthquakes to the attractive powers of bodies.

This was the most wonderful of all the essays. Clarissa read:

"We often see two bodies approach each other without being impelled by any external force. The cause which produces this effect is called Attraction, or that principle whereby the minuter particles of matter tend towards each other. . . . By this is most satisfactorily explained the motions of the

Heavenly Bodies. . . . These spheres, separated from each other by immense intervals, are united by some secret bond. . . . This power of attraction is in some degree the cause of the juices circulating in the capillary vessels of plants and animals. . . . The Supreme Wisdom manifests itself in the government of the Celestial bodies, and is equally apparent in that of Rational Beings."

Clarissa read quickly, with odd little mispronunciations in the long words, and with pauses now and again between the phrases, wrinkling her forehead and staring at the book, as she tried to follow the course of the stars swinging through those vast spaces, united by that secret bond.

Agatha's mind was not bent starwards. Here at last was the great scientific truth which lay behind the appearance of Clarissa. It was the body of Agatha Bodenham herself which had attracted those minute particles of matter from which had been compounded Clarissa's exquisite little form, and then, from those particles, by a perfectly normal law of nature, a rational being had come into existence. It was difficult to understand, but there was no doubt that Clarissa could be explained by the very same law which accounted for the appearance of the planets in the sky and the vegetables in the garden. She had her place between the stars and the cauliflowers.

Agatha never before had considered herself as possessed of any peculiarly attractive power, but now she learnt that it was the attraction exercised by her own body which had drawn Clarissa to her, and had given her life. She blushed uneasily.

They sat pondering, each absorbed in her own thoughts, till Clarissa said:

"I wonder what would happen if one of the stars went just a tiny bit too far away, and got out of the attractive power of the sun."

"It couldn't," Agatha answered quickly, "That's impossible."

"But suppose it *did,*" Clarissa insisted.

"Well, I expect it would just go out," Agatha said, "but it couldn't really happen. That secret bond between them cannot be broken. It said so in the book."

"It *does* happen sometimes though," Clarissa went on; "but they do go out, just as you said. I mean shooting stars. They must have broken the secret bond, and I expect that's why I always feel so dreadfully miserable when I see them disappear."

"Don't think about them if it makes you miserable."

"But it's rather a lovely kind of miserableness, too. I like it."

And then an idea suddenly struck Clarissa, and she went on:

"Oh, I've thought of a new game. Such a good one. Let's play Stars. You be the sun, and I'll be a star that *nearly* gets away, *almost* a shooting star, but not quite. Come on, do let us begin."

"I don't quite see how we should play that," Agatha said doubtfully.

"Oh, I'll show you. It's quite easy. You must go round and round in the middle of the lawn, and I shall go round and round the outside. We can make a thread of your blue silk into the secret bond. That would be perfectly invisible. But if I get too far away, it will break, and I shall go out. It's a really exciting game, because we shall never know what might be going to happen."

It made Agatha terribly giddy, this new game. She held a reel of blue silk in her hand, and slowly revolved in the middle of the lawn, trying to look and feel like the sun, but really both looking and feeling like a very wobbly top, coming to the end of its spin. Clarissa raced round the edge of the grass, every now and then suddenly dashing a few feet out of her course, saying she was attracted by another star. Agatha's part was to anticipate these deviations, and to counter them by letting out a few extra feet of silk before the thread broke. But Clarissa was too quick for her at last. She had thrown herself so entirely into the spirit of the game that she was longing to go out like a shooting star, and all at once she gave a very unexpected swerve, and the thread was broken. She turned head over heels, and disappeared into the kitchen garden.

"Oh, oh, oh! I was attracted by the earth, and I've bumped my head against it, and I've gone out," she called, and then was perfectly silent.

Such a long time passed, that Agatha grew frightened, and ran to look for her.

She was lying quite still, her head hidden inside a large flower pot, which she had pulled over on to its side.

"Clarissa, darling, get up. Are you hurt?" Agatha said breathlessly.

There was no reply.

"Clarissa!"

It was a cry of real anguish.

Clarissa tilted the flower pot, and looked out, opening one eye roguishly.

"It's no good calling me," she said. "I've gone. The secret bond is broken."

Agatha tried to laugh.

"I thought you had really hurt yourself," she said.

"Oh, no, not a bit," Clarissa sang, and she jumped up and danced away across the lawn, with the flower pot on her head. She looked like a very mad toadstool, and Agatha really laughed this time. She couldn't help it.

They spent all their days like this—reading together, playing together, and sometimes inventing new games, like the Star Game, from the books they read. Agatha was supremely happy, so happy that she felt there must be something sinful about so much happiness, and she wondered if it was selfish of her to keep the child so entirely to herself. Ought Clarissa to be encouraged to lead a more normal life: to play with children of her own age, to share their games?

She silenced these doubts by remembering that as a child she herself had had neither the desire nor the opportunity of playing any game but the game of Clarissa. Other children expected too much of her, the spirit of competition, the power to hit a ball or to run a race. They had always made her feel inferior, out of it. But she sometimes thought that Clarissa was cleverer than she had been: indeed, she often seemed to excel just where Agatha herself had often failed.

So the first time that Mrs. Burns, the rector's wife, came to call after Clarissa's arrival, and brought her Kitty, her little girl of eleven years old, Agatha was relieved to find that Clarissa sat close beside herself, surreptitiously clutching and squeezing her hand, and staring at Kitty without saying a word. Mrs. Burns suggested that the two children should run away and play together, and then Clarissa showed great de-determination, and said in firm tones:

"Please let us stay with you. We like it much better than running about."

The guest didn't agree, but had to acquiesce.

After this, Kitty was sometimes asked to tea. At first Clarissa found her as difficult to play with as a spade and bucket, and Agatha had to amuse them both. This was difficult, as she was not naturally amusing, and moreover the two children did not care for the same things. But as time went on, they became used to each other; and spent long, long afternoons gardening together in Clarissa's garden, and making tea for themselves and for Agatha in the little garden house.

Agatha watched with mixed feelings the growth of this friendship, if friendship it could be called. Perhaps Clarissa showed herself to be more really human in developing a power of getting into touch with other people, and yet—Agatha was tortured by jealousy. Till now, Clarissa had breathed, moved, and lived, only and entirely in sympathy with herself. She hated to lose a moment of her time, a word that she spoke. She wanted to keep everything.

And it was not only jealousy, but *fear*, lest Clarissa should somehow slip away.

She might go out, like a shooting star.

VI

Agatha was doing her accounts when the policeman came to see her. He had been a familiar figure to her all her life, but she had hardly ever spoken to him, though she looked on him as an old friend. Her closest acquaintances were generally people whom she knew by sight, and had known by sight for years. She felt at ease with them. They belonged to her landscape. She liked the postmistress, and the parish clerk, and the butcher and the other village people, because among them she knew her bearings. With strangers she felt at sea. But neither with strangers nor her village intimates did she consider much conversation necessary.

Agatha turned to receive the policeman's visit, feeling faintly surprised.

They greeted with friendly courtesy.

"I understand you have a little girl living here with you, Miss, an adopted child," said the policeman.

Agatha stiffened a little, and slightly bent her head.

"I have called in to ask you to be so kind as to fill up this paper," the policeman continued. "By law these details have to be notified to the authorities."

Agatha took the paper he offered. It was divided into columns with spaces to contain certain information. She read:

"Name of infant. Place and date of Birth. Name and Address of Person from whom the Infant has been Received."

"No, I cannot do this," she said, handing the paper back. "I can't fill in those details. It is too complicated."

The policeman laughed kindly.

"That's just what we feel about all these

Government papers, don't we, Miss?" he said. "There's a lot of red tape, as the saying is. But there, we have to do it, and I dare say I can help you, if you'll kindly allow me, and show you what has to be done."

Agatha felt she was losing her head.

"No," she said, with uncertain resolution. "I shall decline to make the statement altogether. No one can force me to, can they?"

"No, Miss, I don't suppose they could. But if you don't fill in the paper, you won't be allowed to keep the child."

"Not allowed? Who can stop me?"

"The law of the land, Miss."

"But what can they do with her? They can't take her from me and turn her into the road."

Her voice was wild.

"She would have to go to the Workhouse, if she had no relations to take her."

"The Workhouse?"

Agatha felt the colour leave her cheeks. It was as if a hand from within had clutched at the blood-vessels. She had been standing. She now sat down suddenly.

"Who can do this?" she said in a voice which sounded quite outside her control. "Nobody can. It is no one's concern but my own."

"I know it seems unnecessary, Miss," the policeman said, "and, of course, in the case of a lady like you it is only a formality; but the law has to be the same for all, and no one is allowed to receive an adopted child without the same being registered according to the Act. It is done in the interest of the little ones themselves."

"I have the interests of this child entirely at heart," said Agatha, with a tinge of haughtiness. "I do not expect the Board of Guardians to point them out to me."

"Certainly, Miss. No doubt of that, I'm sure. This paper is quite formal, but I'm bound to ask you to fill it up. Shall I just jot down the particulars, if you will kindly give them to me? and then you will only have to sign your name in the place indicated."

He produced a fountain-pen, and spreading out the paper on the table, he turned to Agatha.

"We want the child's name, with date and place of birth, and the name and address of the parties from whom you received her—her previous domicile, in fact."

Agatha was perfectly silent. She was completely unprepared for this. What she dreaded when Clarissa first appeared had been the kindly curiosity of her household. She thought embarrassing questions might be put to her, either by her old servants, or perhaps by the Rector, or Mrs. Burns, or some other of her rare visitors. But she had comforted herself by the knowledge that no one could really compel her to speak of Clarissa's antecedents, and that no one was intimate enough with her to be entitled to her confidence. If she did not choose to talk, there was the end of it. And now, without any warning, while her head went round and round, she heard the policeman's voice, expressing no impertinent curiosity, but with the dead certainty of a Government official who knows that he cannot be denied, calmly saying that there was a legal authority which could take Clarissa away from her. Clarissa might be in the Workhouse. This was the penalty of living: you came within reach of the relentless arm of the law.

The policeman was as much taken aback by Agatha's silence as she was by his words. Ladies like Miss Bodenham generally accepted very naturally the regulations of the authorities. They did not try to evade paying their dog licences: they called at the office in person to pay the duties on their male servants. He waited, staring awkwardly, with the pen in his hand. She sat still, looking down at her hands which were clenched together in her lap. Her mind was blank. She did not know what to do.

Suddenly she spoke.

"She is a love-child. She is my own."

And when she had said this, she began to cry.

"A love-child." The phrase had surged up from her inner consciousness, and she spoke it without realizing what it implied. It just did express what Clarissa truly was to her—the creation of the love of all her being. It was the truth, and in face of the truth she knew that no one could take the child away. She had saved her.

But at what a cost! Her position, her name, her character—she had given them all, but Clarissa was hers, hers with a right which no law could override.

Yet, when she heard the words actually spoken, she realized for the first time their import and her own shame. She, Agatha Bodenham, had by her own words disgraced herself in the eyes of a common policeman. So she heard her sobs—and they sounded like the sobs of someone else. She knew she had no pride left to restrain them.

Strangely enough, the policeman felt that the humiliation was his, not hers. To himself, he seemed the one who had blundered. Greatly embarrassed and most apologetic, he gathered up the paper and put it into his pocket, murmuring:

"Excuse me, Miss. I beg your pardon, I'm sure."

Agatha pulled herself together. The policeman's attitude had brought the situation back towards the normal.

She rose and led the way into the hall.

An enchanting picture met her eyes. Clarissa had dragged out the library steps, and had climbed them to reach some attractive-looking old books on a very high shelf. Perched cross-legged on the highest step, she balanced on her knee an enormous book bound in old red leather, and as Agatha and the policeman came through the doorway behind her, she swung herself round, with an air of impish triumph, and held the book high over her shoulder to show her prize. It was a gesture from fairyland. She was higher than the level of the window, in the shadow above the light, and her face glimmered like a moth in the twilight.

But she had not fixed the steps securely. The sudden movement was too much for them, and with a great crash they fell to the ground. Clarissa and the big book went down with them.

It was Agatha who screamed, not Clarissa; and then, for the first time in her life, Miss Bodenham fainted.

The policeman caught her as she fell.

There were still tears on her face as she lay motionless, with her hair ruffled and untidy, and her head supported on the policeman's knee. And when the servants ran to the hall at the sound of the crash, what they saw was Miss Bodenham lying in a dead faint with the policeman beside her, and no sign of Clarissa at all. She had completely disappeared.

"More frightened than hurt," thought the policeman, when he looked round and saw she was gone, though when she fell he had had no doubt that she had broken her neck.

They revived Agatha with sal volatile, which she always kept in the medicine chest, although she had never used it before. As she miserably gasped her way back to consciousness, she began to cry again, her dignity all gone. At the moment that she opened her eyes, there was a little sound in the doorway behind her. Policeman and servants looked round.

The tiny face of Clarissa, seeming smaller and more transparent than usual, flitted in the shadow thrown by the half-open door. She looked frightened, trembling, and somehow unreal.

For a second she stood, with a lost expression, as if she did not recognize the place in which she found herself. Then she suddenly ran across the hall to Agatha, and with a passion of feeling which she had never shown before, she threw her arms round her, clinging to her, and covering her face with kisses.

"Where did you go? Where did you go?" Her voice fluttered and failed for a moment—it became almost a sob. "I couldn't see you. It was all dark."

"I didn't go, my darling. I fainted."

"Then you must never, never faint again," and again Clarissa clung to Agatha, squeezing her hands, and pressing them against her own face, as if to make sure they were both alive.

The memory of Clarissa's falling figure slowly returned to Agatha's consciousness.

"But, my darling," she said, "tell me, where

are you hurt? It was that terrible fall of yours that made me faint. I was so frightened."

"Hurt?" Clarissa was puzzled. "I wasn't hurt. That noise wasn't me falling. It was the ladder."

"But you fell with it, my treasure."

Clarissa almost laughed.

"The noise didn't touch me," she said. "But it must have hurt the ladder I should think. It was such a crash."

"My little girl looks very white now, though," said Agatha.

"Because you do, and I was frightened in the dark when you were gone. It was so dark that I was lost too. Don't talk about it. Let's forget it."

VII

The policeman made up his mind to tell nobody what happened in his interview with Miss Bodenham, and, as he always said, to the best of his belief he never spoke of it. Yet somehow it was soon known all over the village. News is like that: it flies on its own wings.

He did mention it to the servants in the kitchen. They spoke of Miss Bodenham's emotion as being entirely caused by Clarissa's tumble, and before he knew what he had said, the policeman betrayed that she had been crying before she went into the hall. Having gone so far, he was obliged to say why she was crying—in self-defence, for he did not want to appear a bully. And then, Miss Bodenham's own servants ought to know the truth; they probably knew it already.

He regretted his words, for the business-like Helen at once possessed herself of his paper, and discovered from it that he had no right to worry Miss Bodenham at all, these particulars being only asked for in the case of foster-parents who received children for pay, "which of course a lady like Miss Bodenham would never think of doing."

And then Helen's eloquence broke forth.

She told the humbled policeman that all this trouble had come about because, like many another man, he hadn't got enough to do, and must needs make a job just to make himself important. She would like to know what the Guardians would say if they came to know that he had been interfering, with his impudence. And it was no wonder Miss Bodenham had been upset, and had told him what she did just to teach him to mind his own business. And it would be like his foolishness to swallow down what she had said, when she was only giving him the set-down he deserved.

And much more than this did Helen say, till the policeman fled, beaten and ashamed, with no inclination to open the subject elsewhere.

And when he was gone, Helen and Sarah and the Cook found themselves faced with a dilemma.

They knew Miss Bodenham well enough to be certain she would never say what was untrue. But they were equally certain that she had never had a baby. It seemed impossible to escape from one or other of these alternatives. To accept either was disloyalty to Agatha.

There was nothing to be said. They separated, and went about their work.

It was really a good thing that Miss Bodenham had fainted, and that Clarissa had had a tumble, so that Helen could treat them both as invalids, and so cover up the embarrassment felt both by Agatha and herself when they next saw each other.

Agatha didn't know what the policeman might have said, and Helen didn't know what Miss Bodenham thought he might have said. It would have been an awkward moment, but Agatha really felt ill. She wanted Helen's ministrations, and was grateful for smelling salts, eau-de-Cologne on her forehead, and a cup of clear soup to drink. It comforted her too, to smell the embrocation with which Helen insisted on rubbing Clarissa on the places where she ought to have been bruised.

As a matter of fact, she wasn't bruised anywhere, but she, too, liked the smell of embrocation, and the pleasant feeling of being fussed over.

By nightfall, Agatha almost felt as if nothing had happened before Clarissa's accident, but that this had given her such a shock that they were both ill.

In the morning, she awoke to the memory of the terrible thing she had said to the policeman. How could such a phrase have fallen from her lips in the presence of a man? How could it have been in her mind at all? She remembered she had heard of gently nurtured ladies, who, when delirious, broke into coarse and blasphemous language such as they could never have heard in their lives. She could not analyse the state of mind from which those words had come. Certainly she had hardly known what she was saying. It had been an inspiration from without. Nothing else could so completely have silenced the policeman and paralysed the arm of the law. She had spoken as one possessed—but possessed by God or by devil?

From whatever source, she accepted with unutterable relief the sense of safety which had succeeded that supreme menace; and she was too remote from her neighbours even to be aware of the gossip which raged about her for the next few weeks. There was a special flavour about this scandal, because nobody believed it, however often it was repeated. The thing was unthinkable. To look at Agatha was to know that the policeman's story was an impossible one, and yet its very impossibility made it the more amusing.

The Rector and Mrs. Burns were much distressed by all this talk. Like Miss Bodenham's servants, they did not know what to think, and together they discussed the characters of Agatha and Clarissa. It was true that, although she had lived always in the Parish, they knew nothing at all about Miss Bodenham. Nobody did. She was certainly secretive, and yet it was inconceivable that she could ever have had a secret to hide.

On the other hand, Clarissa's appearance had been mysterious. Agatha had never said who she was, or whence she came. It looked as if there might be some disgrace about her birth, and possibly she was the illegitimate child of some relation of the Bodenhams; but if so, it was still very strange that Agatha, who saw practically nothing of her relations, should have discovered this little waif and given her a home.

Mrs. Burns was uneasy. She said one never knew what unpleasant characteristics might develop in a child of unknown antecedents, and she wondered if Clarissa could be a safe companion for her little Kitty.

The Rector would not listen to this. He did not believe in heredity, and pinned his faith to the power of education and environment. He thought no harm could come to a child brought up in Miss Bodenham's house, in spite of the character she seemed to have given herself to the policeman, who, after all, was a stupid old fellow, and had probably misunderstood the whole thing. As a clergyman, he declared that he looked upon Clarissa as a child of God, and he asked no more questions as to her parentage.

Meanwhile, on this very point, Agatha was enduring a new ordeal. Going into the garden one morning, she found old Hunt in tears. His only daughter was married to a shepherd, living in a remote cottage on the downs, about fifteen miles away. She had just had her first baby, and now after two struggling days of life the little child was dead, and dead unbaptized. The village clergyman had said that the Burial Service could not be read by the grave of the non-Christian child—the Prayer Book forbade it. And poor old Hunt leant on his spade and wept, the tears running down his cheeks at the thought of the baby in the unblessed grave.

Agatha was filled with pity and concern. She was sure that Mr. Burns would not have been so severe, and she wanted to hasten to the Rectory and ask him to intercede with the clergyman.

But, to her surprise, Hunt would not think

of this. Hard as he thought the sentence to be, he accepted it. He acquiesced without rebelling.

"No, Miss," he said, "What's done can't be undone. 'Tis too late to make amends once the breath be out o' the body. That's where do lie the responsibility of bringing children into the world. You'm got to mind their everlasting salvation, and if the parents don't mind it, the children won't be worthy of it. The sins of the fathers be visited on the children, no mistake about it. That's God's law, and you can't alter it."

"But your daughter wasn't to blame," said Agatha, aghast. "Living so far way as they do, there wasn't a clergyman within reach to christen the baby."

"They could 'ave done it themselves, and they did ought to 'ave done it. Why, even a woman be allowed to do that in case of need. I can mind the nurse as nursed my mother, she christened my little brother, 'twas the last my mother had, just afore he died. Did it in the teacup, and 'Innocent' was the name she gave him. The only one I ever knew called by that name, and he were gone within the hour. But he were a Christian, as much as you or me, and that's what my daughter should 'ave seen to. It means eternal life or else everlasting damnation."

Agatha went into the house. Her theology was unable to refute Hunt's arguments, though her heart indignantly rejected them. And yet, perhaps he was right. At any rate, no one could take any risks in face of such an appalling possibility.

And, as ever, she was thinking only of Clarissa, who also had never been baptized. But had she an immortal soul at all? Could there be within her—wisp of the imagination as she was—anything which could ever inherit eternal life?

She could not find ease of mind by consulting Mr. Burns, for she was afraid he might ask questions which would be as difficult to answer as those of the policeman, and she could not face that, but neither could she face the possibility that her sinful neglect might send Clarissa to everlasting punishment. And then there came the thought that even if Clarissa were as yet without a soul, who could say that the act of baptism might not be the new birth through which one would be given to her, and with it, the gift of immortality.

Agatha saw that, like the nurse of old Hunt's mother, she must baptize the child herself.

She waited till Sunday came, a day when the house was very still and quiet, and all the servants gone for their afternoon walk. Then she called Clarissa, and dressed her in the dress she had worn when she first appeared: it was the only white dress she had. She took the little girl by the hand, and led her into the study, shutting the door behind them. The room was less used than any in the house. After Mr. Bodenham's death, it had been more or less shut up. The blinds were kept permanently lowered, so that the carpet should not be faded by the sun, and when Agatha, as a child, had sometimes softly opened the door and looked into the room, its perpetual twilight, and the long rows of old books lining the walls, had made her feel she was looking into another world, and not only into another room. It had grown to have the sacredness which clothes the objects that have been treasured by the dead.

Clarissa had brought an occasional movement of life into the study, for she used to run into it to find books, but she and Agatha never sat there, and now when they entered the room together, she felt awed, knowing that here was something beyond her comprehension. They stood together beneath a large framed photograph of the Sistine Madonna, and Agatha put her arm around the child, and bending over her, she told her that the time had come for her baptism, when she would be made a child of God, and an inheritor of the Kingdom of Heaven. Her voice trembled, for she was profoundly moved, and she was also very nervous over what she was about to do. But it was a fervour of love which shook her, and which, while it shook her, gave her the power to surmount her agitation. Before her mind there stood the picture of that little baby, denied a Christian burial, and perhaps enduring endless punishment for the sins of its parents. Clarissa was solemnized—thrilled—impressed. She stood very still, holding her breath and closing her eyes, while Agatha read from her Prayer Book the words of the Service for the Private Baptism of Infants. She held in her hand a shell, which legend said had been picked up on the shore of the Sea of Galilee by Mrs. Bodenham's godfather, and when she reached the words of Baptism, she poured a stream of water from the shell on to Clarissa's forehead. It rushed over her, falling down her cheeks, and dripping from her hair, her eyelashes, her nose, and her chin. The sudden cool shock made her gasp. She quivered and turned pale. There was a vibration, as though some new life had indeed entered the room, and for a few moments Agatha held her clasped in a wonderful stillness. Then she kissed the little face, and felt the fresh cool water on her lips.

That kiss of Agatha's brought Clarissa back to earth.

"Let me do it now," she said. "I want to christen you, too."

And she was disappointed, and rather unconvinced, when told that this was something which could only happen once in a life.

But Agatha was marvellously light of heart when they went into the garden together. A weight was lifted off her: she felt confident and safe.

"Shall I have a Christening Cup, like the one you have got in the plate cupboard?" Clarissa asked.

Agatha said she should have a cup, or a knife and fork, or a Bible, or any other present she chose, as a memorial of her baptism.

Clarissa skipped about, thinking what she would choose, and Agatha sat, completely at peace, her hands lying idly in her lap, watching the child, and listening to her intermittent talk. For a few minutes Clarissa was out of sight, playing near the gate into the road, and then she reappeared, running very fast, and with her face aflame.

"I know what I want for a christening present," she called, as soon as she was near enough to speak. "God has sent it here this very day."

Agatha went to meet her.

"Come to the gate quickly, quickly," Clarissa was saying. "There is a poor little monkey outside. It's very ill, and I'm afraid it's going to die. The boy is too poor to keep it warm, and I want to buy it from him."

"But Clarissa, we can't have a monkey."

Agatha was frightened of all animals, dogs, bulls, and mice, and a monkey was outside her range altogether.

Clarissa had taken her hand, and was hurrying her along. She was talking very fast, and she really did not hear what Agatha said. She was sure that God had sent the monkey to them, so that she should, on the very day of her baptism, do a good deed and save its life. It was better than any other christening present, because it was alive, and it must have come because she was now a Christian and must help God to take care even of the little sparrows which fell out of their nests.

Agatha thought that a sparrow and a monkey were two very different things, and yet she did not like to repress Clarissa's zeal. It seemed to prove that those minutes in the library had indeed given her something which she had not possessed before, something which must be cherished and developed, and because she was convinced of this, Agatha had to consent to buy the monkey from the boy with the organ who was standing at the gate.

It certainly looked a most miserable little thing, lying in the boy's arms, with its crinkled whitish eyelids almost covering its eyes, and with its long-fingered hands doubled up like the wings of a sleeping bat. Agatha thought there was no doubt that it would die very soon.

But it didn't. Clarissa saw to that. She wrapped it in warm flannel; she fed it with hot milk; she carried it in her arms all day, and, in spite of Agatha's protests, she insisted on its sleeping with her in her own bed that night.

Far from dying, it recovered very quickly, and by the next evening it was so lively that no prayers of Clarissa's could vanquish Agatha's disgust and persuade her to let it sleep with Clarissa, in their joint bedroom, for another night. It was given a warm basket with a rug and a cushion in the back kitchen, and fastened by a chain to the leg of the table, so that it could not run more than a few feet.

Clarissa decided that the monkey's name should be Poppet, and she was deeply wounded when Agatha refused to have a Baptism Service in the study for it, like Clarissa's own. On this point, Agatha was firm. Such a thing would be a profane parody of what had meant so much to her.

Poppet attached no more meaning to the syllables of its name than to any other sound. It never came when it was called, and this was a grief to Clarissa, while Agatha minded more that it so often came without being called. It was a whirlwind in her sedate house, breaking her china ornaments, spilling the milk and the ink, and tearing the silk hangings with which the piano and the mantelpiece were prettily draped. It was dirty, too, and the servants detested it. It knew no law and obeyed no authority. Agatha hated its hideous, miserable, grinning human face, which seemed to her to degrade the race of man, dragging it down toward its own apish level.

And she was very frightened of the monkey, too, when it ran across the room on all fours, dragging its lead behind it with a rattling noise on the floor, and sometimes, when it was angry, it chattered and hissed and showed its teeth in a very wild way. Yet Agatha was touched and charmed when she saw Clarissa carrying the monkey about, holding it tenderly as if it was a baby, and playing with it as other little girls play with dolls. But when Clarissa's attitude was most exquisite, bending caressingly down, with her head a little on one side, and a bewitching smile on her face, suddenly Agatha would see beside this charming picture the horrible face of the monkey looking up at the little girl, like a diabolical caricature.

The six months of Poppet's life in Miss Bodenham's house were therefore far from pleasant ones, and when the monkey succumbed to an attack of pneumonia soon after the cold weather began, Agatha felt greatly relieved. It seemed disloyal to Clarissa, who was heart-broken and cried terribly, though she was somewhat comforted by arranging a very ceremonious funeral, when Poppet's coffin was followed by a procession of inwardly joyous mourners, in the shape of Agatha, old Hunt, Reggie, and the indoor servants. A tombstone was placed over the grave, with these two lines inscribed on it:—

POPPET
A PET

Clarissa persisted in thinking that this was a poem, or at any rate a very good rhyme.

They returned to life alone together. Agatha feared that Clarissa would mope without her pet, and would miss the monkey which she had carried in her arms wherever she went throughout the past few months. But the memory seemed to pass completely from her. She never spoke of Poppet, although she loved gathering wild flowers on her daily walks and making them into wreaths which she laid on the monkey's grave. This seemed to be an end in itself, having no connection with Poppet; and when Mrs. Burns warned Agatha that she feared Clarissa was in danger of becoming morbid, Agatha well knew that there was no danger of that. Clarissa lived in the present; she did not recall the past.

To the outside observer, their lives appeared very dull. They saw nobody except the Burns family, with whom they sometimes went to tea, while it became a rule that Kitty should come and play with Clarissa every Saturday afternoon.

When autumn came, they returned to the hotel at Brighton for a fortnight of sea air; but they made no new acquaintances, and never spoke to the other guests.

But as they walked together, they were full of animated talk, absorbed in each other, regardless of the world about them. People often wondered what they could find to talk about—that solitary woman and child. No one guessed the stirring adventures through which they lived in the acting games which filled their days. There they were in a boundless world, full of people of their own choosing.

VIII

It was the sixth of June—Agatha's birthday, and Clarissa had always said it was hers too. If she had been, as she thought, eleven years old when she first appeared, she was now seventeen.

So to-day she had done up her hair for the first time, and Agatha's present to her was a turquoise ring, an ornament which she was now considered old enough to wear. They sat in the garden after breakfast, and looked at it on her finger, feeling that it marked an epoch.

A motor stopped at the gate. This was unusual. They had no motoring acquaintances, and and neither of them had ever driven in any motor except the taxi which took them to and from the station at Brighton when they went there each year. This was not really surprising.

It was only a mile and a half to the little country town where they and the other village people did their shopping, and it was a very pleasant walk there, across the fields. If Agatha ever wanted to drive, she naturally supported the village cab, as her mother had always done, and as time passed it grew to look more and more as if it needed her support.

Still, motors played a large part in their lives. In the games they played together, they possessed a very comfortable motor of their own, in which they went on imaginary tours, not only into every part of England, but in France and Italy as well. They had an old chauffeur who was a great character, an obstinate man who liked to have his own way, but was nevertheless a most loyal and faithful servant. He taught Clarissa to drive, and she became a skilled and daring driver.

Still, an actual motor-car was something quite outside their usual experience, and when the car stopped, they neither of them expected that it could mean a visitor. The gate clicked. Kitty Burns ran up the drive.

Her cousin David had arrived last night in a motor, and he was taking her for a drive: she wanted to give Clarissa and Miss Bodenham the birthday treat of both coming too.

Clarissa was delighted, but Agatha thought it the most alarming birthday treat that could possibly have been proposed. David was not a professional driver; he was only a boy, not much older than Kitty and Clarissa. She knew it was most dangerous.

"But he drives splendidly," said Kitty. "He came more than two hundred miles yesterday, and he has won lots of races."

This was the reverse of reassuring. Certainly one would feel less, rather than more, at ease in the village cab if a jockey held the reins, and a racing motorist was a much more desperate character than any horse jockey.

Agatha laughed nervously, and said she would prefer a more steady driver.

Then she saw Clarissa's disappointed face, and knew that she must give in.

Clarissa leaped into the seat by the driver, while Agatha and Kitty got in behind.

The car seemed to go terribly fast, and Agatha's breath was completely taken away by the wind, which then proceeded to battle with her for her hat. She clung to its brim, pulling it terribly out of shape, and feeling as battered as the hat itself. She was watching Clarissa, and thought that she too was enjoying the drive less than she had expected, for she was not looking at the countryside as it rushed past them, but sat with her eyes on the steering-wheel, evidently anxious as to the driver's skill.

After a time, she asked David a question.

"Don't speak to the driver!" shouted Agatha from behind. "You must not divert his attention, it is not safe."

To her horror, David seemed almost to turn round in his seat and look back over his shoulder, as he answered:

"It's all right, it doesn't disturb me at all."

"Don't speak to anyone," cried Agatha.

She tried to control her fears, feeling that they would disgrace her in Kitty's eyes, but it was agony to her to see Clarissa again speak to David, and then he seemed to be explaining to her the uses of the various handles and pedals.

After a time, they slowed down, and Agatha could begin to breathe once more.

"I want to drive," said Clarissa, turning round and looking over her shoulder with a bewitching smile at Agatha.

"No! No! My darling, you can't, you mustn't. I beg you not to. It is not safe."

Agatha knew she was making a fool of herself, but she couldn't help it. It was a matter of life and death.

"Do let her try," said David. "I will keep

my hand on the wheel, and I promise you it will be quite safe."

"I forbid it," said Agatha. She had never spoken so strongly to Clarissa in her life.

Clarissa was alarmed at her vehemence.

"Of course I won't if you feel like that," she said, but she looked a little sulky. It was the first time that their wills had ever been opposed. A cloud fell over them, and David drove on.

Clarissa was bored for a few moments, but very quickly her interest returned, and she was obviously learning all she could from David, even though she did not actually drive. In fact, there was a time when she did put her hand on the wheel, and helped to steer the car, though David still controlled it.

Agatha pretended not to see. She said no more.

They drove for about two hours, and when they got home Agatha jumped out quickly, and hardly waited to say good-bye. She ran into the house, and up to her bedroom, where she was violently sick. She was reeling.

Clarissa stayed for a few minutes at the gate, saying how much she hoped that Agatha would let her learn to drive. David and Kitty were surprised at her ardent desire for this, and at the spirit with which she was ready to take the wheel without demur on the very first time she had ever driven in a car. They could not know how long she had in imagination been an expert driver, and that therefore it seemed to her the natural thing that if she was in a car at all, she should drive it.

When Agatha and Clarissa met at luncheon, it was easy to see that their drive had affected them in very different ways. Agatha's face was the colour of sand, and her usually neat hair was draggled and untidy. She looked shattered —exhausted—broken. Clarissa, on the other hand, had more colour than she had ever had in her life. Her hair had fallen out of the tight round chignon into which she had so laboriously pinned it that morning, with the help of Agatha and Helen, and it was now gaily and merrily blown about. Her eyes shone, and she was full of new zest and enthusiasm.

"I must learn to drive," she said. "Do please let me, and then let us have a motor, so that I can drive you about. We will make our play real."

"Playing at motoring is more to my taste than motoring itself," said Agatha primly. "I didn't like it at all. It made me sick."

Clarissa couldn't believe it.

"You will soon get used to it, and love it as I did," she said.

"Never! I did not like the motion. I hate the noise, the shaking, and the wind. In our game, we can drive without any of those inconveniences."

"But we have none of the fun, either."

"Imagination takes us much further than anybody's motor-car can go."

To Agatha this sounded unanswerable.

"But it's so futile only to pretend," said Clarissa.

It was only by a great effort that Agatha could save herself from bursting into tears.

"Yet how much pleasure you and I have always had from pretending," she said. "Are you never going to play our game again?"

"Of course I don't mean that," said Clarissa. "I shall always love it. But if we really did the things we play at, they would be even more fun. I never thought it was possible before, but now I see what a lot we have missed."

Then Agatha saw that she was too old for Clarissa.

She went upstairs and lay down on her bed, trying to master her troubled thoughts.

Over and over again she heard in her mind Clarissa's words, so unconsciously cruel—

"What a lot we have missed . . . it's so futile to pretend!"

And yet, Clarissa had been as entirely happy as she had herself. Agatha knew it as she looked back over the past six years. And she was aware, as she lay there, that she was indeed looking back on them as on to something that was over. She was recalling an atmosphere out of which she had already moved.

Strange that on the day when Clarissa was supposed to have grown up, Agatha should for the first time have learnt how much younger she was than herself—younger than she had ever been, and that she should have known that it was this spirit of youth which had broken in upon their peace.

Agatha had enjoyed the acting games, in which she and Clarissa passed practically the whole of their lives, because, through all the stirring adventures that they imagined together, there ran the serene certainty that they were all the while in a world where the events were entirely under control, where there were no surprises, and no disasters which did not bring their own remedy. Clarissa, on the other hand, had found in them her nearest point of contact with the real world of adventure. She had thrown herself into them perhaps more completely than Agatha, and they had satisfied her because she almost believed they were true; but now at one touch of the outer world, she had understood that what she wanted was life itself.

Slowly and painfully Agatha came to see that she could only keep Clarissa by going with her. She wished to do real things. Well, she should do them, but Agatha must share them. Hitherto, the course of their lives had been entirely directed by Agatha, and as long as she led, nothing ever happened. They did nothing; only played at it. Now Clarissa would be the guiding spirit, and it appeared that she would at once step out of the artificial world which Agatha had created for them to live in, and go to the everyday world which had always been so comfortably and remotely outside, a world which seemed to Agatha at once more commonplace and more disconcerting than their own.

She dreaded it, but when she came down to tea, her mind was made up. Still, their wills should be one, and that will—Clarissa's. For Agatha knew, in spite of the terrors she had suffered in that motor-car, that she really dreaded nothing in the world but the breaking of the union between herself and Clarissa. She could face, and even enjoy, everything that they did together.

IX

"I expect you thought me very stupid this morning," Agatha said, as they sat at the tea table, eating birthday cake; "but I was not well. The car shook me a good deal, and we must remember that it was my first real long drive. I should enjoy it more later on."

Clarissa's face lit.

"I am so glad you will try again," she said. "I do want you to like it as much as I do. I can't really enjoy anything that you hate."

"I shall not hate it," said Agatha, "but I should feel safer driven by a really good professional driver, like Jenkins." (Jenkins was their imaginary chauffeur.)

Clarissa slipped her hand under Agatha's arm, and leant against her, looking very sweetly up into her face.

"Do let me learn to drive," she whispered.

Agatha would not appear agitated.

"Yes, I think that you would drive very well some day," she answered, "but I am nervous, you know. I can't pretend that I'm not, and I should insist on your learning from a real chauffeur, and not from a wild young man."

"I wonder who we could find to teach me."

"No one here," said Agatha firmly. "I should wish you to have the best lessons available, and I think you will have to take them in Bath."

Clarissa jumped up and danced about the room, and Agatha, watching her, for some reason recalled the first time she had ever appeared, when she had run away down the long green path and had vanished at the end. She had that same look of fleet youth.

"It's lovely, lovely!" she was saying. "And it is kind of you, when I know that really you don't a bit want me to learn. But I believe you will love it when I can, and then we will have a motor of our own, shan't we? And I can take you for all the expeditions that we have played at. Oh! What fun it's going to be."

It seemed to Agatha that she had parted for ever with her peace of mind. Where would this wild progress end? But for Clarissa's sake she had resolved to go through with it, so she answered with an attempted gay serenity:

"Yes, darling. When you can drive it, we will have a motor of our own, but you must be a completely skilful driver first."

Then began a fortnight of torment for Agatha. Every other day they went to a School of Motoring in Bath, generally driven there in David's car, for he was enthusiastic over the lessons, and not at all hurt because he was not considered a "safe" teacher. Agatha suffered tortures during the drive, which was fifteen miles each way, and she hid from Clarissa the horrid fact that she was sick regularly every evening when they got home. She managed to control herself when they were actually in the car, though once she was obliged to fly from the tea table at Fortt's, and lie down for nearly an hour, before she was able to face the journey home.

Clarissa was not a quick learner. This was something completely unlike anything she had ever attempted before. She had never even used a sewing machine, and she was frankly puzzled by the big engine—the gears, the clutch, and the brake. The engineer who taught her had an unfailing flow of words—most of them unfamiliar ones, by which he fluently explained the technicalities of driving to her, and Clarissa listened to them with humble attention, but could seldom see their connection with the handles and pedals in the car. Agatha secretly hoped that she would after all find it too difficult to learn, and she fancied that the teacher thought so too. Her hopes were vain, for Clarissa was bent on being able to drive. On the days when she had no lesson, she spent the mornings in the coach house at the Rectory, sitting in David's car, and there she practised gear changing, and the use of the brake and the clutch pedals, without starting the engine. She did this for hours at a time. Anyone else would have been bored, but not so Clarissa. Imaginary journeys in a real, though stationary, car, were one step more realistic than the motoring games she had played with Agatha, and she could be perfectly contented driving a car that never moved. The games of make-believe in which she had spent her life had given her the art of being happy wherever her imagination could work. So she sat contentedly in the garage, changing the gears of a motionless car, and Agatha began to hope that her motoring would not take her farther than the Rectory stable yard. That was the kind of motor journey she herself preferred.

David and Kitty could not understand Clarissa's frame of mind. They were both exasperated by Miss Bodenham's eccentricities, and they wanted to persuade Clarissa to take drives with them, and to practise on the road. It seemed to them insufferable that Clarissa's activities should be limited by Miss Bodenham's capacities: that because *she* was sick in a moving car, Clarissa must sit in a stationary one; because *she* was afraid to drive herself, Clarissa could not learn on the road; because *she* wanted to keep Clarissa to herself, Clarissa must go nowhere without her. They boiled with an indignant pity which Clarissa neither expected nor desired. She felt none of the inhibitions for which they lavished on her their enthusiastic sympathy. When they stormed and rebelled, she laughed, saying she was just like Miss Bodenham herself, and knew exactly what she felt; and she honestly thought them lacking in imagination when they could not understand her enjoying her drives in the garage.

They came and talked to her when she was sitting in the car, and it was a new thing to Clarissa to find herself enjoying the society of her contemporaries. Up to now, she had known no one of her own age except Kitty Burns, and to tell the truth, Kitty was not very interesting. The two girls were used to each other, but they had never become intimate, and their afternoons together had been rather an effort to both. The arrival of David and his motor gave them an interest in common, but it was really David himself who filled the mornings in the coach house with interest and fun. Clarissa thought him an adventurer from the days of Queen Elizabeth. He was striking looking, lean, and urgent in figure, with very dark hair, and the eyes of a hunter—eyes that have searched far distances. He had been in places with names that sounded to Clarissa like magcial spells: Mwaulo, Mbanga, Isombo, Bisagra, and it was wonderful to know that he had seen these places with his own eyes, had seen the strange tropical plants growing in them, had heard their wild beasts roaring round him in the night, and had not only fancied what they would be like.

And when David talked, Clarissa was thinking of only what he told her: she hardly looked on him as an individual at all. Like Agatha, she had no desire to make friends, she didn't think about that. David was the porter who opened for her the gate to the Kingdom of Reality, and she looked past him into a new world.

It was a world, too, far more amusing than her own. David had a funny, farcical mind, seeing incongruities and paradoxes and comical contradictions all around. He found unexpected absurdities in things which Clarissa had always taken for granted—the people in the village and their customs, so that every day was all at once much more fun. Life was full of things to laugh over.

Miss Bodenham felt it would be unsuitable on her part to spend hours every day sitting in David's motor-car in the coach house. She would have liked to do this, but she was afraid of what the Burns family might think. She hated Clarissa to go off there without her, and she was constantly finding some excuse for running over to see her in the car. She disliked hearing the young people chattering as she drew near, and chattering too in what seemed a rather senseless way; and still more she disliked hearing Clarissa laugh at this nonsense. It was silly, and even vulgar. They were often quite noisy. Peals of laughter were heard in the garage.

She said nothing, but David and Kitty were quite aware of her disapproval, and when she appeared the conversation always seemed to change; it fell to a lower key. Agatha knew this, and disliked it particularly, for it seemed as if there had been something to be ashamed of. Really, she had merely recalled them to her own regular level, for her awkwardness in society always made other people shy and awkward too. Her presence in the garage put on to the others that restraint which always characterized her social relationships, but what made her feel it as a new thing was that Clarissa, for the first time, had escaped outside this restraint: she had found touch with other people, and Agatha was tortured by the contrast.

She began to hate David and Kitty, knowing that they looked on her as a wet-blanket, and though she knew that Clarissa was not with them in this, she suffered acutely when she thought that they probably believed her to be so.

Agatha saw only one way out of it—a painful way, even a terrible way, but the only escape. Without more delay, she must buy Clarissa her own motor. She must take this new interest of hers and make of it something which they two possessed together without anyone else intervening. Then Clarissa would be able to sit in their own garage, and would be under no obligation to David. There would be no need for the other two to come and sit with her, for Agatha would be there herself. A desperate remedy, but there was no other.

Clarissa's delight was unbounded. She guessed at no hidden motive in Agatha's mind, although it was almost unbelievable that she should so soon have accepted the idea that they should own a motor. Evidently, Clarissa thought, Agatha was beginning to enjoy these drives to Bath so much that she wanted to be able to go further afield.

"Of course you won't be able to drive it for a long time," Agatha said. "But we will get the School of Motoring to send us a very skilled chauffeur who can bring it here, and stay to drive us about, and he can continue your lessons."

The project entailed one more long day in Bath with David and Kitty. Clarissa wanted them to come to help to choose the motor, and Agatha herself thought it was as well to have a man for the occasion, and a man who understood something about the different types of cars which she believed were in existence, who would know what questions to put, and would see that they were not being cheated.

So they all went off for the day. The drive was torture to Agatha as usual, and in fact it was even worse than usual, for she felt she was driving to her fate, and she could not foresee what that fate might be. Clarissa too enjoyed driving in David's car less than she had done, for when they were on the road, she realized that, in spite of all her practising, she was quite incapable of taking control in the open, when there was any possibility of their meeting anyone. She felt a failure, but she hoped that it would perhaps be quite another thing when the motor was their own, and the new chauffeur had taught her.

But they all enjoyed Bath. Agatha herself was excited when she found she was actually buying a motor-car. The cars all looked so new, so important, so comfortable, so brilliant with varnish, and so luxuriously upholstered. Clarissa was on tiptoe with excitement, and sprang into every one that they were shown, to try the driver's seat. There she sat, a pale little form in a pale dress, silhouetted against the firm unyielding sweep of the powerful lines of the various cars. David was completely master of the situation, and carried out the purchase in a manner that Agatha was obliged to admire; while Kitty felt that the whole transaction was due to her having introduced the Bodenhams into the motoring world.

Buying the motor took all the morning, and then they went to Fortt's for luncheon. For the first time, Agatha began to think that she might some day agree with Clarissa that doing things together would be even more wonderful than imagining them. Lunching in a restaurant, for instance—the food was not a bit like what they had at home. Really Agatha liked it less, but it came as a surprise, and this gave it character. Clarissa thought it great fun to study the bill of fare with the other two, and to order dishes with mysterious names, without having the least idea of what they would be like. She ate ices, too, several of them, more than any of the party. She looked a most fairy-like little being, and yet she had always been able to eat more than Agatha, and she never had a touch of the indigestion which always coloured the tip of Agatha's nose and the points of her cheek-bones, as well as giving rise to other uncomfortable symptoms if she ate anything rich.

They went to a concert in the Pump Room.

Agatha enjoyed the music, but still more she enjoyed gazing at Clarissa's face as she drank in the harmony of the Mozart quartette, and watched the movements of the players. There was rhythm in the very poise of her head, in the lines of her figure, so flexibly rigid, and in the way her breath came through her parted lips.

It was a new thing to her to listen to music, to follow the intertwining melodies, and to feel the completeness of the chords as they fell upon her untrained ear, and she seemed to have found something she was waiting for. It was as though a very delicate little instrument had been slowly and exquisitely created, chased, and polished, the strings wound round the carved ivory keys, and then tuned, tuned, tuned in some silent workshop by a spirit worker: and now, all of a sudden, a bow was laid across the strings, and the first low tone drawn from them.

"She is my instrument," thought Agatha. "The music within her is mine. And now it is being called out, articulated: and she and I hear it together."

Her eyes drew Clarissa's to themselves. They

were always conscious of each other's gaze.

Clarissa turned and brought Agatha into the softly lit circle of her happiness. They shared it. The other two were left outside. To them, this was an ordinary concert, one of many, and they were the ordinary commonplace listeners. Agatha and Clarissa found a new closeness of communion, hearing together for the first time the music of Mozart.

And it increased Agatha's happiness to know that in this experience Clarissa was the leader. Alone, she would not have felt the music: it had never meant much to her. Clarissa was sensitive to impressions, as she herself had never been, and through Clarissa, she for the first time felt the thrill of being touched directly by the sheer beauty of sound.

And then she began to remember that all the beauty that she had ever found in poetry and in books had been shown to her, too, by Clarissa. It was Clarissa who had read it all to her. All had come to her in the tones of that little thin low voice. Tears filled her eyes.

In the evening they sat together and talked about their day. They forget to play their usual game.

"What a wonderful day it has been," Clarissa said. "We are going to be even happier than we have been before. Our motor will take us everywhere—miles and miles away, and we shall often hear music together. I wonder why we have never been to a concert before."

"We enjoyed it far more than the others, who have heard so many," Agatha answered. She couldn't bear Clarissa even to suggest that perhaps they had wasted time in the past six years. If it came to that, what about her own thirty-eight years without concerts. She did not regret them, for she knew that now she possessed all in possessing Clarissa. Clarissa was her Eternity—that supreme simultaneity which holds all the wonders of time. Her only wish was that Clarissa should feel this too. Whatever new experience the day had given her, she seemed to have tasted it already in her love for Clarissa. All that happened to her could only show her, in ever new and changing lights, the treasure that was already hers.

X

They drove every day in the new motor. The chauffeur was a steady man who appeared completely to understand Miss Bodenham's nervous disposition, and she could not help feeling at ease when he drove them about the country roads at the quiet pace of fifteen miles an hour. Agatha was glad to observe, too, that he shared her lack of confidence in Clarissa's driving powers, and he agreed that the young lady must have a good many more lessons before she could be trusted to take control of the car. But Clarissa loved learning for its own sake, and she really would have been afraid to drive alone. So she sat contentedly by Jenkins (as the chauffeur most surprisingly turned out to be called), and she only attempted to take the wheel when she saw the road very long and straight and empty before them.

It was true, as Clarissa had foretold, that on these excursions, they were happier than they had ever been before. Everything that happened to them fell into place as a scene in their old game of fancy, but they found that real life had a far more fertile imagination than theirs had ever been. Things were constantly happening which they would never have thought of inventing. Their sedate drives were full of surprises. They had never laughed so much in all their lives as they did when they found themselves in Devizes on a market day, watching pigs being driven through a crowd of country people, and then had luncheon in the inn among farmers, who talked loudly and very racily. This was indeed seeing life, and a side of life which they had never pictured in their play in Miss Bodenham's drawing room.

But Agatha could not help feeling rather

annoyed when Mrs. Burns told her that David was to be with them for five months. That was the length of his leave from the Sudan, and as his father, the Admiral, was in China, he was to make his headquarters with his uncle and aunt. Mrs. Burns hoped that Miss Bodenham would allow Clarissa to see as much as possible of her young people: life in the country was usually so very quiet, and it was an opportunity to have this young cousin with them.

David insisted on marking out a tennis court, not only at the Rectory, where one generally appeared in the summer, but also on Miss Bodenham's soft and mossy lawn.

Agatha could hardly believe it when Clarissa asked to be allowed to buy a racket so that she could learn to play tennis. She had never thought of such a thing before, though Kitty had often asked her to come to the Rectory in the morning to play singles with her. Games had bored Clarissa as much as they bored Agatha, but this summer she suddenly felt the desire to throw herself into all sorts of unwonted activities—to try to do things for the mere delight of doing. And although she had no more actual gift for tennis than she had for driving a motor-car, yet she showed a natural gift for learning, or rather, for being taught, for she was not a quick learner, only an attentive pupil.

Agatha watched the tennis lessons. Clarissa stood in the court, listening with eyes and lips, as well as with ears, to the instructions of her two teachers. A little crinkled frown appeared at the top of her nose, and her face wore a puzzled, absorbed look. With the utmost docility, she closed her fingers one after the other upon the handle of her racket, in search of the correct grip; she planted her feet exactly as she was told, first carefully studying the example, and then bending over her own feet, and very deliberately placing them in the exact position, she swung the racket with the prescribed movement of the body. And a far more exquisite swaying movement it was than that of either of her teachers; but she did not often hit the ball, and she hardly ever hit it over the net.

Exasperated as Agatha was by the constant society of David and Kitty, she felt bound to admit that it was very kind of them to take so much trouble to teach Clarissa, as the lessons must interfere very much with their own games. Then one day she saw suddenly that it was not kindness at all. It was something else—something which she had never thought of as a possibility.

Love.

Clarissa never could learn the right way to hold her racket. She held it lightly as if it were a wooden spoon with which she was whipping cream, or a feather broom dusting the ornaments. She tried to copy what David did, but as soon as she put one finger in the right position, she moved all the others, and the racket again slipped about uncertainly. David came round the net, and taking Clarissa's hand under his own, he put her fingers one after the other into place, and held them there. It was then that Agatha, sitting beside the court, suddenly saw his face. At the touch of Clarissa's hand, something stirred in him and about him. It was indefinable—like the vibration of the air seen across a field on a hot summer's day. It changed him. Agatha knew that in that moment he was aware only of Clarissa: he had forgotten the game of tennis.

Agatha was not observant. She very seldom saw anything till it was pointed out. But this she saw more quickly than anyone else could possibly have divined it. She was immediately aware of an emotion in David which was akin to her own. He, too, wanted to possess Clarissa. Agatha hated him.

The colour rushed into David's cheeks, and

at the same moment it left Agatha's. She felt as if he had drawn it forcibly from her.

She looked at Clarissa, agonized to see how she bore herself in the suddenly tense atmosphere, and she saw that she was as unmoved by it as was the tennis racket, in which she was still entirely absorbed. It was unbelievable that anyone could be so completely unconscious of the fact that she was in the centre of a whirlwind. That was how it looked to Agatha.

But as David took his hand away, Clarissa was only looking at her own fingers as they clutched the racket. She was absorbed in the effort not to move them. She wanted to impress upon her memory, and, if only she could, upon the very handle of the racket itself, the exact position in which her hand was now clenched.

"Oh, Kitty, serve a ball quickly," she called. "I want to hit it now, when I've got the racket exactly right at last."

For Kitty, too, nothing had happened outside the sphere of racket and ball.

She served. Clarissa missed the ball.

"Am I still holding it right?" she asked in urgent tones, holding her racket across the net, to be inspected by David, who had gone back to the opposite court.

Agatha saw that he had the grace to be embarrassed. He obviously couldn't tell whether Clarissa was right or not.

Agatha got up quickly.

"It is getting late," she said. "Clarissa, we must come indoors and get ready for dinner."

A swift glance passed between her and David. They knew that they were antagonists.

Thinking it over in the evening after dinner, while Clarissa was very serenely and delicately lifting specimens of pressed flowers with a pair of tweezers and putting them into her book, Agatha felt rather foolish. As she tried to remember it, she realized that literally nothing had happened. She looked at Clarissa, and knew that for her there had been a tennis lesson and nothing more. What was it then that had sent Agatha into such a fever? Merely a fancied expression which had passed over a face, an expression which now she could not recall. No word had been spoken. Nothing had happened which had not probably happened many times before on the tennis court.

And yet she knew that she was not mistaken, and the memory of the silent look which she and David had exchanged when they parted assured her that he too knew that, though no no single thing had changed, yet the whole world was changed—the world in which Clarissa moved, calm and unconscious, herself alone unchanged.

Agatha remembered that she had somewhere read that in the very centre of the wildest typhoon there is a space of perfect stillness, round which the whirlwind rages. In some such crystal globe of peace, she seemed to see Clarissa—aloof—apart—while the storm tossed Agatha's soul and David's. Fiercely they would fight for her, she all the while so beautifully unconscious of the battle.

It seemed impossible the next day to believe that things could go on as if nothinig had happened, but everything was as usual. Agatha and Clarissa drove in the morning, and after luncheon there was tennis, and much chattering and conversation between the games. Agatha sat stiffly by, her eye fixed on David, looking like a very awkward and inexperienced spy. She most obviously kept him under supervision, and he was as obviously aware of this. It made them both ill at ease.

David felt it so much that he was driven to all sorts of expedients to try to get Clarissa out of Miss Bodenham's sight, and away somewhere with him, while Agatha was equally bent on circumventing his tactics. Silently they played their game. Agatha won, for she had Clarissa as an unconscious partner. She didn't at all want to be carried off by David, and had no wish for a *tête-à-tête;* but Agatha found the struggle terribly exhausting, and the next day she was in bed with a sick headache. Clarissa wouldn't leave her. She sat by her all day, bathing her forehead with eau-de-Cologne, and soothing her by the touch of her always cool fingers. Agatha was at peace. The headache vanished, but she wouldn't confess it, feeling safe so long as she had Clarissa with her, behind the closed Venetian blinds of her bedroom.

After that, she often had recourse to an artifice which made her secretly ashamed. Keeping David and Clarissa apart became a mania with her, and it was a terrible strain. Every two or three days she pretended to have headaches, and thus kept Clarissa to herself. These days were breathing spaces which enabled her to live.

David resented them keenly.

"It is intolerable," he said to Mrs. Burns. "Clarissa spends half her life shut up in a dark room, mopping that old maniac's head with a wet rag. It isn't safe. It isn't decent. It isn't healthy."

Mrs. Burns laughed. Like Agatha, she had her suspicions, but they did not perturb her. She thought a love affair at that age was perfectly natural, and led to nothing.

XI

Agatha thought she liked picnics, and in the long winter evenings she often played at going to them with Clarissa. She felt rather differently about them in the summer, preferring them at a distance, like most other things. She often remarked that in this English climate (which she always spoke of as if she had personally compared it with all the other climates of the globe) there are really very few days when it is either pleasant or safe to sit out on the grass to have tea. In all her life, she had only done this three or four times, and had then disliked it quite actively, but in conversation she liked to say how much she enjoyed an alfresco meal.

Mr. Burns was fond of archæology, and he thought that the presence of two motor-cars in the village was an opportunity for him to indulge in his hobby, so he proposed that they should all join in an expedition to the ruins of an interesting medieval castle some miles away, and have tea there. Agatha agreed that it would be a delightful thing to do some day, and if she had had her way, the matter would have rested there, a pleasant prospect, but a distant one, like a romantic view seen from afar.

But since David's arrival, the Burns family never could let well alone, and on the very next fine day which fell far enough from a Sunday for the Rector to feel free from the weight of an approaching sermon, he appeared soon after breakfast, and suggested starting that afternoon. There was no valid reason against it, and Agatha consented.

The morning was a busy one, collecting things and packing them into the motor. Agatha took many rugs, mackintoshes, cushions, furs, and scarves: two camp stools, two white parasols lined with green, as well as a kettle and baskets of food. She prepared for any vagaries of the weather, and she wore goloshes, spectacles of tinted glass, and a large blue veil tied over her hat.

It was a beautiful drive, over downs where peewits turned and tossed overhead, and where long lines of farm horses moved against the large still curve of the skyline. Clarissa loved these wide spaces: she sat silent, staring. Agatha just watched her, she wanted no more distant horizon.

The castle was a fine ruin which had been partly demolished by Cromwell's men, but retained much of its primitive character—a high tower which could be scaled by a half-ruined stairway; a narrow footway round the ramparts, from which there was a marvellous view of the country; and many rooms and passages, roofless, open to the sky. It stood in a wide space of green turf, with a few fine trees about it, and wooded slopes fell from its walls to a lake, beyond which could be seen the eighteenth-century house which had been built to replace the old castle.

David at once went down to the lake to see whether he could find a boat, for he had quickly decided that this would be a good way of getting Clarissa away from Miss Bodenham. Clarissa and Kitty walked about the ruins, while the three elders began to unpack the baskets. Agatha enjoyed this. She liked setting out the cups and saucers, and fussing over laying down rugs and shawls for people to sit upon.

David soon came back, asking for the girls, and saying he had hired a boat.

Agatha saw his purpose, and she determined to frustrate it. With consummate guile, she declared that she herself enjoyed boating beyond anything in the world, and she said she must go too, for she liked nothing so much as a row on the water.

David was obviously much disconcerted. This was a passenger of whom he had never thought, but he could only say that, of course, he hoped Miss Bodenham would accompany them.

The Rector and Mrs. Burns said that they preferred terra firma, and poor Agatha wished that she had been able to admit how completely she shared their taste, but she knew that she had no peace of mind when David and Clarrisa were together unless she made one of the party. She had no confidence in Kitty as a chaperone.

They went to the lake, and looked at the boat. It was small, and not particularly clean. Agatha wondered if, after all, she would dare to face the voyage.

"It doesn't look very safe. Do you think you can really manage it?" she said to David, her heart beating uneasily.

Mr. Burns assured her that David had been

brought up among sailors, and could be relied on to navigate any craft in any water.

"You mustn't come if you feel nervous, Miss Bodenham," said David cordially.

"I am not nervous," Agatha answered, with a complete lack of truth, "and I should be most disappointed at missing my row."

She was determined to maintain her reputation as an ardent lover of boating, so that no one should suspect her real reason for embarking on this alarming and unpleasant expedition.

"Where are the girls all this time?" asked Mrs. Burns, and as she spoke, Clarissa and Kitty were seen approaching from the direction of the Castle.

"Are you and David going for a row?" Clarissa said to Agatha, in some surprise."

"You are coming, too, of course," David said quickly.

But Clarissa wouldn't think of it. She was

frightened of the water, and didn't mind saying so. Nothing would induce her to change her mind. She was quite firm.

"Kitty and I will watch you from the bank," she said.

David and Agatha declared simultaneously that they would not dream of going without her. Neither of them had thought of this contingency.

"Oh, you must go," Clarissa answered. "Please do. I couldn't possibly prevent your having a row just because I'm so stupid as to be frightened myself. It would make me miserable."

And she looked so.

"No. Miss Bodenham must not miss her row," the Rector said jovially. "You enjoy it so much, and I expect you don't often have the chance of going out with such a jolly young waterman as this."

David and Agatha felt like puppets. They

found themselves placed in the boat, and with faces of hardly concealed dismay, they set out on their voyage.

Clarissa threw herself down on the grass beside the lake, and began to show Kitty how to weave a little basket from the reeds which grew at the water's edge. Agatha had taught her how to do this. It was a craft she had learnt from her nursery maid, and now across the water she could catch the curious tones of Clarissa's small voice, and she knew exactly what she was saying without actually hearing the words. She heard her laugh at Kitty's clumsiness, and she could tell just how the baskets were growing—Clarissa's swiftly into shape, and Kitty's becoming a formless tangle.

David could not follow the talk, but he took such a course that, while Agatha in the stern of the boat had her back to the girls most of the time, he could watch Clarissa as he rowed. She was lying full length on the grass, leaning on her elbows, and holding up the little rush basket on a level with her eyes. Her white hands caught the light as she rapidly twisted the rushes, passing them in and out of each other with a sure touch. Then she swung herself round to see what Kitty was doing, and both the girls laughed at the muddle she had made. A moment later, Clarissa had run down to the waterside to pick some more rushes. She stood, pale and nymph-like, in the dwarf forest of green sword-like reeds, and then she moved through them with a wading motion, for they grew so thickly that they impeded her like water as she reached for the tall likely rushes which suited her purpose.

The two in the boat completely ignored each other. David rowed silently, his eyes fixed on Clarissa: Agatha sat still, listening to her. Though she had refused to accompany them, she was still the solitary companion of each. The row lasted about twenty minutes, and they hardly exchanged a word throughout that time, but each thanked the other when they got back to land.

Clarissa helped Agatha to land with real relief. Agatha's desire to go on to the lake had surprised her very much, and had made her vaguely uneasy. She was quite sure that in her heart of hearts Agatha was not happy in the boat, and she was aware of something which she could not understand in the plan of the voyage altogether. She was puzzled and disturbed.

Tea was ready when they joined the others, and then, while Mr. Burns read aloud to Agatha some passages from his Guide Book, describing the historical features of interest in the Castle, the three younger ones drew together, and seemed to be planning something. Soon they moved off.

"Where are you going, Clarissa, darling?" Agatha called.

"To climb to the top of the tower," was Clarissa's answer.

Agatha sprang from her camp stool.

"My dear, it can't be safe. These ruins are terribly dangerous, I know. The stones are crumbling."

"It's all right," Kitty said airily. "Everyone goes up. It's the regular thing."

"Do let us go," Clarissa pleaded. "There is a wonderful view from the top, and we ought to see it."

"If you go, I go too," said Agatha firmly. She saw through David's intention, and it was not only the wish to share the physical danger with Clarissa which determined her to make one of the party.

"I am afraid you would find it rather a climb," the Rector interposed.

"I think we old fogies are safer down here," Mrs. Burns added brightly.

Agatha was deaf to their words.

"Clarissa cannot go without me," she murmured, and leaving Mr. and Mrs. Burns without ceremony, she hastened after the other three, clambering up the broken stairway as fast as her goloshes would allow.

Clarissa looked round and saw her coming.

"Here is Agatha," she said. "Let us stay and help her up."

"Much better push her down," was David's muttered comment to Kitty.

Clarissa had gone back, and was showing Agatha where to put her feet, and how to climb up the somewhat dilapidated remains of the stairs.

The staircase wound up the inside of the tower, and came out, with one last very steep step, on to a passage which ran round the top of the wall. They found themselves very high up, and the parapet was very low. The tower descended sheer beneath them to the green lawn, and all around the country stretched, wide and far away. It was a magnificent view.

Agatha was suddenly giddy. She threw herself down on her face, and was unable to move.

Clarissa was terribly concerned.

"Don't look down, if it makes you giddy," she said.

"I can't help it," Agatha moaned. "We are so high up, that there's no other way to look."

"Then let us come down quickly."

"I shall never be able to go down. Never. I can't move."

She had quite lost her nerve.

Clarissa looked anxiously at David.

"What shall we do?" she asked.

"Don't ask him," said Agatha querulously. "He can't do anything to help."

She lay prone, clutching with her fingers at the stones.

Clarissa could only turn to David, in silent dismay. He seemed to be their only strength.

She was very frightened. All her life she had leant only on Agatha, who had directed the quiet events of their days, and had provided for her in the trifling emergencies of her childhood, and now, all at once, Agatha was helpless. It was she who needed Clarissa now, and at the very moment of her need, Clarissa felt a giddiness creeping over herself, too—not the mere physical giddiness from being there on that height, but something more fundamental, as though her life had lost its inner spring. For a moment she began to feel darkness growing around her, then she realized that she must not let herself go: she must save Agatha, and in David's strength was their one support.

She did not like to speak to him again, as she saw that to discuss the situation only maddened Agatha, but she looked at him dumbly, with those soft brown eyes of hers which held within them such changing lights and shadows, and he silently answered her appeal.

He signed to her that she must try to persuade Agatha to crawl on her hands and knees to the head of the stairs. It was only a very few feet.

She refused to move. Clarissa sat down beside her.

"Do let David help us down," she whispered. "It will get worse and worse the longer we stay up here."

"No, no, it is he who makes it worse," Agatha groaned. She had an idea that if only she and Clarissa were left alone, her courage might return, but when she tried to visualize the actual descent, she clung to the stones where she lay. They seemed the last solid rampart in a swaying world.

But by degrees Clarissa and David did manage to move her—half dragging her along, and half persuading her to crawl— the few feet which lay between her and the top of the stairs. When she looked down, she could not believe that she had come that way. It was not a staircase at all, only the few sloping remains of footholds in the wall. The idea of stepping over the side and down into the abyss was unthinkable.

Then Clarissa had an inspiration.

"Go and fetch Jenkins," she said to David. "He will help us down. He is very sensible."

And sulkily David went to fetch him.

But even Jenkins had great difficulty in persuading Agatha to move, and the whole party sincerely agreed with him when he said that "Miss Bodenham didn't ever ought to have gone up."

There was not room for two people together on the steps, and at last Agatha was conveyed down, with Jenkins holding her from above, and David going down the stairs beneath, taking her feet, and placing them one after the other into position on the broken stairs.

Clarissa and Kitty followed.

The picnic had been a failure throughout, and the exhausted Agatha was at once placed in her motor-car and driven slowly home.

XII

Sometimes in the evening, when Agatha was tired after a long day, she leant back in her chair and shut her eyes, while memories of the past floated vaguely through her mind. Then she often saw the picture of Clarissa dancing. She had always danced when she was a little girl.

That summer when she first appeared, more like a dream or a phantom than a living child, she had come dancing and floating over the ground, as if her feet hardly touched it. In the white dress of those days, she had swayed and curved about the lawn as though a wind from the trees had swept down to bring her, and to drive her about in wayward gracious rhythm. She danced then to her own singing—nursery rhymes which Agatha herself had almost forgotten, and she sang them in a voice as faint as a grasshopper's, till she vanished in her dancing like a bird which is lost as it flies.

Later on, she used to dance in the drawing-room, while Agatha played, with stiff and chilblained fingers, on the piano, which had stood in Mrs. Bodenham's schoolroom. Its keys were yellow, and its tones were thin and cracked. Agatha sat by it, and marvelled at the invention and grace with which Clarissa envolved dance after dance to her playing, for she herself had never been able to dance at all. So Clarissa danced alone, without a partner, and as she grew older she gradually forgot her steps, and played duets with Agatha in the evenings instead.

Kitty Burns often tried to persuade her to come with her to the dancing classes which were held each winter at the High School in the town near by. Kitty enjoyed these, but Clarissa was shy at the thought of finding herself among a crowd of strange girls. She could not face them, and also, she had no desire to learn the modern dances. Both she and Agatha disliked their names, and agreed that they did not sound like dances at all.

But a day or two after the picnic, when they were all sitting one afternoon in the Rectory garden, Mrs. Burns said that she was going to give a dance for Kitty and her friends, and that Clarissa must certainly come to it.

Clarissa said she could only go to a ball if she was allowed to dance by herself.

"I can't think how two people can possibly dance together," she said. "I can only dance alone."

The others laughed at her, but she stuck to what she said, and then, remembering some of the dances she used to invent, she sprang up and threw herself into the old poses, moving over the lawn with winged steps, singing as she went in a little shrill voice that came from nowhere. It was enchantingly pretty, but it would have looked very odd in a ballroom. Kitty teased her, and told her that her dancing was like that of a baby of five years old, but David was enthusiastic, saying it was inspired, and that she was a genius and a born dancer.

Agatha thought it an impertinence on his part even to admire Clarissa's dancing. His praises exasperated her, and she was relieved when Kitty persuaded him to join her in giving a demonstration of a modern foxtrot. She and Clarissa sat together and criticized, agreeing that they thought it ugly.

"Try, Clarissa," said David, leaving his partner, and returning to the other two.

It was Agatha who answered.

"No," she said, addressing Clarissa. "You could never do that. It's not what you call dancing at all."

Clarissa mocked at them.

"I don't want to look like you two," she said.

"You couldn't," David answered, and coming to her, he took her hand as though he meant to take her literally from Agatha's side, and compel her to dance with him.

Agatha pushed him away. She had never done anything so violent before, and she felt at once that her impulse had been unladylike. She sat erect and spoke acidly.

"Don't tease her. She doesn't want to dance with you."

Clarissa laughed lightly.

"As David says, I couldn't," she said, but the next moment she was trying the steps with Kitty.

It was a swallow pirouetting with a porpoise.

David sat down on the seat by Agatha, who hated to know that he appreciated as much as she did the difference between Clarissa's fairy-like movements and Kitty's jogtrot. And yet the two girls somehow kept in step.

"You could soon do it all right," Kitty declared.

"I can now," Clarissa answered as she sat down, and she was astonished to find that she could.

In the evening she and Agatha talked of the proposed dance.

"After all, I believe I do want to go," Clarissa said. "I think the actual dances are stupid, though I suppose one could dance them in one's own way; but I do want to know what it feels like to be at a real dance, and I should like to have a new dress to dance in. You must have one, too, and they shall be the loveliest dresses we have ever had. Let us go to Bath and buy them."

Agatha knew that this dance would be a crisis in her struggle with David. In the ballroom he would have the right to take Clarissa from her side, and she knew that she could never consent to sit and watch them dance together. But she did not know what to say. She temporized; thought that perhaps Clarissa might after all not want to go when the time came, but it would be best to have their dresses ready in case she did.

So they shopped in Bath, taking a very long time to decide on what they wanted. For Clarissa they bought a little silvery dress, the colour of starlight, and Agatha chose black lace for herself. They got many other things as well—shoes, stockings, gloves, fans, and flowers, and with each thing they bought Agatha felt that she was becoming more and more hopelessly involved. Each purchase was another link in the chain which would drag her to her defeat.

As the days passed, the dance seemed to become more and more inevitable. Nothing else was talked of. The guests, the music, the refreshments, the floor, all were discussed again and again, and Agatha felt helpless as she heard how entirely Clarissa had accepted the prospect of going and how naturally the others expected her to be there.

And worst of all, the tennis lessons gave place to lessons in dancing, and Agatha had to sit by and watch David with his arm round Clarissa's waist, showing her the different steps, and she saw that Clarissa seemed to find it quite easy to dance with him, as though they understood each other and moved naturally in step.

But when at last the evening of the dance arrived, Clarissa was once more sitting by Agatha's bedside, bathing her throbbing forehead with eau-de-Cologne. And on the ottoman at the foot of the bed, in two large cardboard boxes, the two new dresses lay swathed in their tissue paper.

The throbbing in Agatha's tortured head grew less by slow degrees, and her breathing gradually became snoring. She was asleep. For some time

Clarissa sat motionless, watching her, and then, very quietly, she put the bottle of eau-de-Cologne back in its place on the washing-stand, and went and stood by the open window.

XIII

Like Agatha, David had known that this evening would be the turning point in their struggle. He knew that when he danced with Clarissa, he must at last have her to himself, and that they would speak to each other alone, away from Agatha's watchful antagonism. But as the time passed, and all the guests arrived except the two for whom he was looking, he slowly realized that he was once more frustrated. Agatha had won again.

The Burns family met together indignantly to discuss what they should do in face of Miss Bodenham's cruelty in depriving Clarissa of her first dance; and Kitty determined that she herself would run over to find out what was the matter, and to insist on bringing Clarissa back with her.

“No,” said

was that in h

to do anything

It was only

Rectory to Mi

went down the

music of the

gradually faint

garden, he seem

enchanted circle

world. The gard

light of a yellow

stood out alone

ground which by

colours. The white

as the moon hers

poured scent out of

wide lips.

David moved nois

shadow to shadow

trees which parted th

e-Child

n going.” And there

made it impossible

ards from the

, and as he

vened, the

growing

ed the

o an

her

sed him

or not he w

he found

to her v

Then

for at

and h

came out into the
The moonlight shone
n like crystal, and in
ng white surface, the
nham's room showed as
ainst the darkness in the
could see Clarissa stand-
shone upon her, lighting up
g it a spirit-like transparency.
watching him, but her eyes
ook of a sleep-walker, and she
ble that she might have been a
tue.

e nearer to her, a sense of awe
n, so that he hardly knew whether
ould dare to speak to her, and when
himself beneath the window he called
ry gently indeed.

he saw that she was glad to see him,
the sound of his voice she swayed slightly,
er lips parted in a faint smile, but she did

not speak. There was less tension in her attitude, however, and it seemed to him that it must have been fear which had kept her rigid. He had frightened her, coming up like that through the trees, and he cursed himself for his clumsiness.

Then he called again, and this time a little louder—

"Clarissa, come down. They have sent me to fetch you."

Still he got no reply, only a small helpless gesture which seemed to indicate that Miss Bodenham was there, asleep, and must not be disturbed.

Though he realized that this would, of course, prevent Clarissa from speaking, he was nevertheless aware of a strange element in her silence. It was as though she were a very long way off, and not the Clarissa of every day.

"Something has happened," he thought. "That woman is a vampire. She has put some spell upon Clarissa. There's something uncanny in her power," and with all the fervour and passion that was in him, he called her once more, putting all the strength of his love into his voice, and determined by that strength to save her and to draw her to himself.

This time he knew that he had reached her, for she moved quickly forward, and for one horrified moment he thought she was going to step out of the window and come straight to him in answer to his call. He sprang forward to save her as she fell, but she turned back again into the shadow of the room.

He waited, listening.

The door opened slowly, and Clarissa stood on the threshold.

"I have been so frightened," she said, and her voice shook as the stars shake on a misty night. "Agatha is asleep, and I have been lost. I thought I was awake alone."

The flood of moonlight all around her seemed

to dazzle her, and she reeled as if she was about to fall. He caught her, taking her hand, and was startled by its icy coldness.

"You must be ill," he said. "Is your hand always cold like this?"

"It used to be," she answered, and drawing it from him, she held it out towards the sky. It was transparent in the moonlight.

"Clarissa, little one," he said, and with all the tenderness of his nature, he tried to pierce the strange mist of dream which seemed to enfold her, "Clarissa, I have come to find you. Have you forgotten the dance?"

"The dance?" she cried, and her face lit with its own bewitching smile. "Oh, oh, the dance! We are going to it. Oh, we should be there!"

Her torpor fell from her, and with a magical lightness, and a poise instinct with gaiety, she sprang past him and moved across the lawn with some of those exquisite fairy steps which she had created in her childish dances. For a few seconds she floated here and there in the moonlit circle of the lawn, and then he saw that she was going further and further away from him. He followed, fearing he knew not what.

She flew like the shadow of a cloud in the wind. Nothing could equal the silent fleetness of her footfall, and when she reached the garden gate which led into the lane, she laid one hand upon it, and flew over it, as if she had wings. It did not arrest for one moment the swiftness of her flight, whilst David, following her, found that the object delayed him for a second or two.

Clarissa danced down the road before him, and now the music of the violin could be heard faintly through the night.

"Oh, oh, the dance! The dance!" She sang, and her voice rippled with the twinkling leaves of the poplars in the hedgerow, while her feet caught the rhythm of the music.

She sped through the Rectory garden, and reached the window of the room where they were dancing. Here she stopped, and crouching under a tree-fuchsia which grew against the house, she gazed into the room. The passing shadows of the dancers played across her tiny white face, while her eyes caught the reflections of the lights from the candles. She was listening to the music, and she looked past the moving figures to watch the players. The notes of the violin carried with them the pure spirit of dancing. From its strings came a melody which soared and leapt and swayed; while beneath its free and joyous music, the piano kept a steady conscientious syncopated rhythm, as though to tether its floating companion and hold it to the ground.

Then Clarissa spoke.

"I could dance with that violinist," she said. "He knows my dances—listen."

She caught the gaiety of the tune, and was

suddenly all animation. She sprang to her feet, and he watched her, thinking she was going to begin to dance again, but at that moment the music stopped and all the dancers moved simultaneously towards the garden. Clarissa glanced round, startled, and then she flew up the walnut tree like a cat. She crawled along a branch and looked down.

David swung himself up after her and stood against the trunk of the tree. He was bewildered, dazzled, enchanted; every moment more entirely in love, and yet she baffled him. What was she? Not a child, for she was seventeen, and taller than Kitty: not a girl, for she floated like a feather, and flew into trees like a bird; not a spirit—she was human to the touch. But to-night she was all made of mischief and magic, remote from him, and yet calling him to her, to share her elfin mood.

From behind her, he watched the various pairs of figures moving about the lawn, finding the chairs which he dimly remembered himself having placed, in the long bygone past of the very morning, in various sequestered spots about the garden. Such obviously sequestered spots, too, they now seemed to him, as he looked at them from beside Clarissa in the hiding-place of her choice.

They did not speak to each other. Two people were sitting under the tree, and the least whisper would have been overheard; but he could feel the dimple in Clarissa's cheek, and the light in her eye, though he couldn't really see either. Remote in some ways, as she had seemed this evening, yet, as he compared her with the ordinary human beings below, he knew that she was infinitely nearer to him than they were. Each of her wayward movements had touched him with a sympathy closer than any understanding.

The people below were talking about a tennis tournament in which they both seemed to have played, and their conversation was very boring. He thought he heard a little sigh from Clarissa, and then, as if possessed by an imp of mischief, she stretched her whole length along the branch, and lying there in her white dress like a ray of moonlight, she dropped a walnut on to the lap of the girl sitting below.

The two partners looked up. David pressed himself close against the trunk of the tree, merging himself in its shadow, and Clarissa lay quiet as a moonbeam.

"I believe there's a squirrel up there," said the young man below.

Clarissa dropped another nut, this time on to his upturned face.

"Shall I climb up?" the young man said.

"No, certainly not," was his partner's reply. "You could never catch a squirrel, and you'll only spoil your clothes. Let us come away, or we shall be covered in walnut-juice."

She got up and moved off, for she was wearing a new dress.

Almost immediately the music began again, and everyone went obediently towards the house.

Clarissa dropped to the ground, and for a moment she stood still listening to the music. Then she turned to David.

"We must go home," she said, swiftly and furtively, and she sped away across the garden. Again he had that sense of being baffled. There was a distance between them which it seemed impossible to bridge. Hitherto Miss Bodenham had always been with them, keeping them apart; but now, when at last he was alone with Clarissa, she herself held him back from speaking.

"This is all like a dream," she said, as they went down the lane. "I can hardly remember how we came, but I am glad that I saw the dance, and heard that violin," and, in a voice far away like an echo, she sang a few bars of the music they had listened to.

Now they were back in Miss Bodenham's garden, and he knew that what he meant to say must be said quickly, or she would be gone. She seemed tired all at once. There was no more of that effortless floating, when she had barely seemed to touch the ground. Now she walked slowly and wearily, as if she were in pain.

"I have got a stone in my shoe," she said, and sitting down on the white seat, she took off her shoe and shook it. The stone fell on to the grass with a little thud.

Before she could put on her shoe again, David took both her hands and held her firmly, turning her slightly towards himself, so that they faced each other on the bench. She sat very still, expectant. A little breeze passed by, bringing the scent of flowers. It stirred Clarissa's hair, and when it reached the border beyond it touched the blossoms and set them swaying.

For a moment he faltered. Words were too clumsy to express his meaning, and he feared that speech would shatter the delicate dream which surrounded them. Then, overmastered by his passion, he broke out, speaking now rapidly, now with hesitation, but caring not how he spoke if only he could make her understand and respond to the fervour of his love.

"Clarissa, you mustn't go in till I have told you something, something which I cannot keep from you any longer. I love you, darling. I love you with all my heart and soul and strength. You did not know this. Have you guessed it, I wonder?"

She was silent, and he felt her try to draw her hands away from his.

He would not let her go.

"We have been happy together this summer, haven't we? And now this wonderful night is the first time we have been alone together. Did you know that, Clarissa? And did you know how I have wanted to speak to you before?"

"We have often spoken to each other," she said.

"Not like this," he answered quickly. "Agatha has never allowed me to speak to you alone. She wants you for herself. But Clarissa, my darling, could you ever imagine that someone else beside Miss Bodenham might want you, long for you, know that his life was worth nothing at all to him if you didn't share it. Clarissa, my love for you is all that I am now. I simply don't exist except in my thoughts of you, my love for you. There is nothing else there. You are mine—me—you belong to me. You must belong to me, because I love you so."

His voice quivered, and he felt her quiver too.

"Don't, David," she said. "Don't say that. I can't belong to two people, and I am Agatha's."

Agatha again! Would they ever escape her? She haunted them even in this hour which he thought he had stolen from her.

"Agatha?" he cried despairingly. "Agatha! You think she can't live without you, but she can. Of course she can. And . . . I can't."

His voice broke. Clarissa trembled.

"But can I live without her?" She faltered.

"Of course you can, my darling. I shall be with you. We shall be together, and I will be all that she has been, and far, far more. Think what it means if you say No. Soon I shall have to go away. My leave is nearly ended, and unless you will come with me, I shall have to go out of your life altogether. We shall lose each other. All this will be over. I can't face it. Can you?"

"Don't go," she whispered.

"You mean that you do want me?"

She said nothing, but he felt a slight pressure from the hand which he still held in his.

"As I want you!"

"Don't go," she repeated, and her voice was fainter and very piteous.

Then he took her into his arms and kissed her. He had not known before how little she was—how light. There seemed to be nothing there.

But as he kissed her face, her head fell forward on his shoulder, almost as if she had fainted.

"You aren't angry with me, darling, are you?" he asked.

"David!" Her voice sounded all at once as if she were a very long way off. She drew her head back and looked at him, and the moonlight on her face made it all the more spirit-like. She seemed to be reaching towards him from another world. He held her eyes with his passionate, fervent gaze.

Then, with that child-like directness which was always so lovely in her, she took his head between her hands, drew it to her, and kissed him with all her heart. He knew that she was his.

At that moment a sharp cry struck upon the stillness of the garden. David started, and turned quickly towards the house.

The open window framed the figure of Miss Bodenham, standing in her nightgown, with dishevelled hair. The light was full on her face. She looked like one who has lost everything, and who stares frantically into a gulf wherein hope is drowned.

And as that cry was heard, Clarissa went. In one moment she had been beside him, slim and silver, like a ray of the moon; and in the next, she was lost. The shadows had swallowed her.

Once more David and Agatha were face to face. They stood still and stared at each other for an appreciable space of time, and then she went back into the room. He waited, but she did not come down.

As he turned to go, he saw that Clarissa had

left her shoe behind her on the seat. He picked it up. It was a little red shoe, so small that he could scarcely believe it could ever have been worn by anyone but a child of ten or eleven years old.

"I shall keep this till I see her again," he thought, and he put it into his pocket.

XIV

Clarissa was gone.

Agatha knew what had happened. She had seen her go out, like the flame of a candle, and now the light of the moon fell coldly on to an empty space, which a second before had held that clearly defined little figure. She knew that it was possible for a star to escape from its orbit, and so to break the secret link which held it to its sun. It was true, as Clarissa had once said, that shooting stars do go out; the earth has called them to it, but it can give them no life.

Agatha turned back into the empty room. She sat down on her bed and waited. She listened. Hours passed. Now and then a night bird flew by outside, crying harshly, but there was no footstep in the house. Clarissa did not come, and

Agatha knew that she would not. Instead, the morning came slowly, relentlessly, cruelly, into the room where Agatha sat alone, her face greyer than the dawn, her hands colder than the fading moonlight. She stared across the room at Clarissa's empty bed with her nightgown laid out on it, and at the two cardboard boxes, which held the ball dresses. She never thought of looking for Clarissa, of calling her. She waited, and knew that there was no one to wait for, that there never could be anyone to wait for again, and yet that she must always wait.

The clock struck the hours, one after the other. Agatha did not hear them. She simply sat there.

And so Helen found her sitting when she came in with the tea and hot water at seven.

"Miss Bodenham has had a seizure!" was her first thought, and putting down her tray, she ran across the room, and put her arm around the rigid figure. The expression in Agatha's eyes frightened her—helpless, senseless misery—dumb and inarticulate. Then she looked at Clarissa's bed, and saw that it had not been slept in. She realized that this was something worse, more terrible, than illness. What dreadful thing could have happened in sight of those haunted eyes?

"Sarah! Cook! Come quickly. Something awful has happened," she called.

They didn't know what to do, those distracted servants. Agatha was their first thought, and they got her into bed, trying to warm her hands, and giving her hot tea to drink. She said nothing, but now a few tears began to fall down her colourless face—slow, unmeaning tears, which she seemed unaware of, for she did not try to wipe them away. She allowed them to roll out of her eyes, which still stared hopelessly into vacancy.

The scared women sent for all the men

within reach—the gardener, the doctor, the rector, the policeman, and then began the fruitless search for Clarissa. There was no trace left. No clue to follow.

Agatha could tell nothing. She lay insensible to all that passed around her. David was closely questioned, and could only say that Clarissa had disappeared into the house as soon as Miss Bodenham was seen at the window. He was quite certain that Agatha had killed her. He knew that she was demented, out of her mind from jealousy, and before his mind there rose ghastly pictures of the terrible struggle in Agatha's bedroom, when Clarissa's tiny thread of life must have been squeezed out of her by Agatha's maniacal fingers on her throat. For if she hadn't murdered Clarissa, what had happened during the night to send her out of her mind?

Yet there was no sign of a struggle, and it was impossible for Miss Bodenham in her condition to have disposed of a dead body. Some other solution must be found.

But the days rolled past, and none was forthcoming. Agatha slowly reached a condition more or less like her normal one, though the mention of Clarissa's name again brought those heavy hopeless tears from her eyes.

The Doctor questioned her very kindly. So did Mr. Burns.

She only shook her head, saying, "She is gone. Don't look for her. She can't come back."

Whatever had happened to Clarissa, it seemed to be something which had stunned Agatha's will into a deadly acquiescence and her mind into oblivion.

A week later she came downstairs and asked to see David.

He found her standing in the library, a room he had never entered before, and in the unknown surroundings, she, too, was someone altogether unknown. She was revolting—terrible, and yet there was something of grandeur about her, a grandeur which she had never before possessed. She had grown thin, and the bones of her face had almost the dignity of death. The skin was drawn over them with an unnatural whiteness, so that the face looked almost like a mask, and in this mask were set eyes which seemed to have been torn from a living face and maddened by the torture of their tearing. He had never observed Agatha's eyes before. They had been merely episodes in a face that was practically featureless. If he had thought of them at all, he would have said that they were pale and without colour. Now they suddenly appeared much darker than he remembered, but in their darkness were flecks of light which in a horrible way recalled the serene dappling of Clarissa's fawn-like eyes.

Her hair looked dirty and unbrushed, and her brown dress was put on carelessly, hooked into the wrong places, so that it hung unevenly about her meagre shape, strained in one place and loose in another.

David shuddered when he saw her. He felt repulsed, revolted. Yet he knew that from this mad woman he must try to wrest the secret of Clarissa's whereabouts. For the police did not believe that she was dead, and now David too had come to think that Agatha had hidden her, and that he might in this interview succeed in leading her unwittingly to betray the mystery of the hiding-place. It was horrible to think of Clarissa in the power of the maniac who stood facing him, perhaps being slowly starved; at any rate, imprisoned in some unimaginable hiding-place—dark, dirty, suffocating.

He stood waiting for her to speak, and for a few moments she was silent. Her miserable eyes looked past him, hunting in vain through the empty room for the figure that was gone.

Then she spoke, vaguely, and as if to herself, hardly addressing him:

"I saw you that night. . . . Clarissa went. . . . She went. . . . You did it. . . . Why don't you tell them that you know what happened? Why do they all ask me?"

David was completely bewildered. He answered her very gently:

"But I have nothing to tell. I only wish I had. I have been searching for her—we all have—but no one has seen her since she went to your room that evening."

She looked at him vaguely.

"No. It was not in my room. It was in the garden. You were with her. The moon shone, and you kissed her. You took her away, and you have lost her, lost my little darling, my precious child . . . lost her. What does the sun do when a star goes out? Can it find it again? Never! Never! Gone into the dark."

He thought her mind was wandering, and he tried to bring her back.

"Miss Bodenham," he said, "try to remember what happened that night. You saw us in the garden, Clarissa and me, and you called to her. She left me then. What happened afterwards?"

"You know as much as I do," said Miss Bodenham sullenly.

"No, for I never saw her after she went into the house."

"She never came into the house."

The words fell with dead finality, and she was silent.

He saw that his appeals were wasted upon her, and he determined to frighten her if he could. He spoke in a changed voice, looking her full in the face, and trying with his eye to hold her shifting glance.

"Miss Bodenham, you must pull yourself together. You know what has happened to Clarissa, and you must tell me. I demand it. The world believes that you have murdered her. Speak and clear yourself if you can."

"Murdered her? Murdered her? Murdered my little Clarissa? Yes, she is murdered, but it is you who did it," and she hid her face in her hands, rocking herself to and fro.

"No, Miss Bodenham, this won't do. You saw what happened that night, and you know that Clarissa loves me. She is mine now, and I have a right to know the truth. I shall find it out. You shall be brought to justice."

"You dare to call Clarissa yours?" cried Agatha, and her face was lit with sudden passion. "Why, you know nothing at all about her. Whence she came, or how. She was mine—mine only. I gave her life to her, and you have taken it away. Oh, the end of it all, the cruel, bitter end. My little Clarissa, he has killed you. Lost, lost, and dead."

She was shaken by her frenzy, and she fell on to a chair, her lips working strangely.

"But they can't shut you up in a coffin," she

muttered. "They will never know where you are."

David was almost as broken as she was. He searched his brain for some new way of appeal, but he could find none. For a moment there was silence, then he turned to go.

"There seems nothing more to say," he said.

"Yes, there is," said Agatha, and her voice was quieter. It had lost its violence. "I asked you to come here because I had something to say to you. You drove it out of my mind by what you said, but I remember it now." She passed her hand vaguely over her forehead, and stopped speaking for a few seconds. Then she said, very slowly:

"I meant to tell you that you must go away—out of this neighbourhood—at once. At once. It is the only hope of her coming back."

David's heart leapt. It was possible after all that Clarrisa might be safe. Agatha had at last betrayed that she could produce her if he were gone away. He answered gently:

"Of course I will go away if it will bring her back. But how do you know that she would come?"

"I don't know it," Agatha answered. "But if you were not here it might be the same as if you had never come."

"Then I will go away," he said. "To-day. Immediately. And I hope that will mean that Clarissa will be free before night."

"It is the only hope," Agatha answered in a voice that was utterly hopeless.

So David went. But Clarissa did not come back.

She had ceased upon the midnight.

XV

Helen stood at the window, watching Miss Bodenham in the garden.

After the first miserable days, Agatha had changed. Instead of sitting still and stunned, staring blankly before her, she had begun talking to herself, calling Clarissa by name, muttering, and smiling. She insisted on Clarissa's place being laid for her at all meals, and her bed prepared at night. She evidently fancied that the girl was still with her, and with her as a little child again.

Now, in the garden, Helen saw Miss Bodenham playing at ball with someone who was not there. She ran about gaily, calling to the other player, throwing the ball, clapping her hands, and laughing.

Then she flung out her arms, and taking an imaginary child by her two hands, she danced her round and round.

Helen's eyes were full of tears.

But when she looked at Agatha's mindless face, she saw that it was quite happy.

FINIS